MODIFIED

Book One of the Manipulated Series

By Harper North

TORMEN**TP**UBLISHING

North, Harper.
Modified

For more information on reproducing sections of this book or sales of this book, go to www.harpernorth.com or www.tormentpublishing.com

ISBN-13: 978-1521976296

10 9 8 7 6 5 4 3 2 1

Contents:

60 YEARS AGO

REF: JD-8486

10 MAR 2087

MEMORANDUM: Resource Security & Mining Settlement Protocols

We are 40 years into the gradual reversal of the Earth's magnetic poles. Our ability to build a flourishing society based on our advanced genetic modification technology has reached its apex. We are now forced to move on to more aggressive innovation to move us into the future. Society cannot move forward without radical change.

To secure the Enhanced Human Coalition's ability to provide rare earth minerals for societal stability and advancement, we are issuing the system-wide development of Dweller mining settlements.

Until now, all Dwellers have been fully supported by the EHC, with little return on investment. This memo is signaling the start of our efforts to build mining operations in each of our mineral-rich underground habitats.

Requirements:

Each settlement will establish a 70% mandatory workforce to work the mines. The remaining 30% will be allocated for operations and security forces.

To ensure a strong workforce going forward, a Dweller fostering system will be put into place. Details of this system will be forthcoming.

All able miners will be required to work 10-hour shifts for maximum production. Dwellers that refuse assignments will be restricted from food allocations and living amenities.

EHC operatives will routinely monitor the development of this program to ensure order and protect our future.

The formation of this Dweller mining system is vital to our ability to maintain our surface infrastructure. Your region is required to have an active mining operation up and running in no more than three years. All equipment has been allocated and is being processed for delivery.

As always, the EHC leadership is at your disposal. Contact our processing division for assistance.

Founder and Director of the EHC

Edward Nejem

CHAPTER 1

Present Day

One false move and that's it. I'm dead.

Sweat drips into my ear as I grip the crumbling ledge of the cavern wall and yank on my too-slack line. My belayer, living it up safely on the ground below, is a lazy, easily distractible, pathetic excuse for a human being.

And, also, my closest friend.

I glance down between my boots. "I'm dealing with a lot of rope up here, Lacy!"

She jerks the line, getting rid of the excess that formed from my rapid ascension up the cavern face. I press my boots against a sturdy rock and lean back, allowing the equipment to secure me in a seated position while I take a breather. After a moment, I dig into the pocket of my cargo pants for a can of spray paint. With one hand, I hold onto the rope and, with the other, I tag a line of green dots along the wall, marking areas with considerable traces of valuable cerium.

The *Leeches,* up top, have us expanding operations and creating newer tunnels, but I don't mind. This part of the mine's not so harsh when compared to the older, muskier areas heavily polluted from excessive activity. The air here is cleaner, no need for an uncomfortable respirator.

A loud, obnoxious bell screeches and Yasay Tulbert, the local mining boss, screams from several tunnels back at some fresh-out-of-the-oven miners that they have to work late for not producing. Ah, the good old days.

"Lacy, I'm ready to dive," I call down.

She grips my lifelines tight. "Got it, Fin."

I draw in a breath, heart pounding. The last thing I want to do is fall fifteen feet down to solid rock just because I have a terrible belayer.

I slide down the rope, air zipping around my face. When my boots hit the bottom, I grunt. Lacy and I strip out of our climbing gear as we get to our lockers. Neither of us speaks as we drag ourselves toward the rusted metal bridge leading back to the older mines, where we can store our tools. Nearly fifty miners, most near to my own age of seventeen, shuffle their boots over the rocks, none of us bothering to push past one another. It's not like we're more excited to be off our shift than on.

"Finley! Lacy!" a familiar voice calls out after the two of us stash our gear and head down the metal stairwell. A skinny, redheaded boy peers up at us and we meet him at the bottom of the metal shaft. Battery powered lamps line the inner workings of the tunnels—the area called *the Slack*—leading to and from the mines. In the dim light, I study the kid's filthy face. His hair is smudged with soot and a black ring circles his mouth from his respirator. He's assigned to one of the grittier areas of the mine.

Lacy smiles. "Hey, Drape." She playfully elbows him and Drape gives us a goofy smile.

The three of us begin our regular march by way of the tunnels and down various metal staircases toward the living quarters. In a group of passersby, two women in burgundy uniforms pass. I stare at them. They're pregnant. They're not showing yet, but the uniform color marks them as light-duty until the time they go to the Oven infirmary to give birth. Days later they'll surrender them and go back to work, never knowing who their child is again.

I wonder if giving up your baby is hard to do?

"Ugh," Lacy groans, staring at the woman. "I'm never doing that."

"It's not like you have a choice," I answer.

"Oh, I'll just *throw* myself down a mining shaft."

I punch her in the arm. "At least we get out of hard labor for a few months."

But what does it matter? In reality, these two, Lacy and Drape, are the only people whom I care to speak to. We've known one another since our days in the Oven. We were all raised in the Oven—a place designed to simply keep new kids alive until they're old enough to work the mine.

"Did you two feel that quake earlier today?" Drape struggles to keep up. He's younger than Lacy and I by about two years, but he's forever right on our tails. Mine especially. He's a pain, but useful to us on occasion. Might as well have the kid around.

"Everyone felt that quake, *Dope*," Lacy says.

Drape frowns and looks to me. "Funny. You weren't climbing during that quake, were you, Fin?"

"No," I say.

Quakes are common now. I've been told that pre-Flip they were rarer, but that was a hundred years before my lifetime. A lot has changed since then, I suppose. Old-timers speak of a simpler past when all of mankind lived above the surface. It's hard to imagine living anywhere but down below, but I envy the Leeches who get to live above ground. I'm a little shaky on the science behind the whole event, but, evidently, it had to do with the Earth's magnetic poles flipping. Somehow it caused the sun to radiate the planet at a greater intensity, along with earthquakes, climate change, and a bunch of crap I don't care to think about. The older folks say it's hotter on the surface, but I wouldn't know.

Without warning, Lacy stops and grabs the railing, the old metal clanging in protest. The other miners continue forward. I roll my eyes, grab Drape's shoulder, and push past them to get back to her.

"What's wrong?" I ask.

She lets loose a loud, exaggerated sigh, "Oh, Finley," she fake sobs. "I'm *bored*."

I frown at her fake drama. "Oh?"

Lacy flings her head back, her long black hair cascading down her back. She shoots me a devilish look with those dark eyes of hers. Her pretty tawny skin has not been tampered with too harshly after what was a considerably easy workload for us— unlike poor Drape, whose pale skin is covered in miner's dust.

"What?" I snarl to make her get to whatever point she's hoping to make.

"I heard a rumor," she sings, swaying her finger back and forth. Drape's lips twist up into a slight smile. I remain serious, as usual.

"And what rumor was that, Lacy?" I ask.

She grips the railing even tighter and hops up, sitting on the fence and clasping her boots together on the bottom half of the railing to keep from tumbling over. Lacy lowers her head and smirks, then shows her teeth like a wild animal. "I heard a new shipment arrived from the EHC."

"The Leeches send anything good?" Drape asks.

"They always do," Lacy says.

I sigh. Sometimes I think our little games are

just that to Lacy—games. For me, it's about survival, not a thrill rush.

The grin on Lacy's lips gives away her excitement about this shipment she's referring to. The EHC usually just sends equipment to mine their minerals, but on rare occasions, when their leaders are feeling friendly, they send down special treats like toys for the kids in the Oven or snacks for the mining bosses. Whatever will make them feel as if they've done great humanitarian aid during their time in office.

For lowly dwellers like us, seeing any of that stuff is highly unlikely, but that hasn't ever stopped my rag-tag gang.

Drape and Lacy eye me, pleading.

"Fine," I say, readjusting the long, sweaty strands of brown hair falling from my bun. Lacy squeals excitedly before I snap a finger to my lips.

Drape grins at me with puppy dog eyes. "If you're going, I'm going."

We continue through the Slack, hiding ourselves amongst the crowd. We walk with our heads high, and without speaking we turn down a tunnel opposite the rest of the crowd. Confidence is key. We act as if we're supposed to be headed this way, like we've been sent on an assignment by Yasay. We come to a metal stairwell and Drape silently points up. Shadows dance across the cavern's surface. Mining guards. We huddle under the stairs, the boots of the guards clinging and clanging over the metal above.

The men speak clearly, no raspy sounds in their breaths. That's how you know you can't trust a person: their lungs are clean. They haven't spent their lives breathing in mining dust. Guards live in a position of privilege. Well, as close to privilege as a dweller can get. I remind myself that there are worse existences than working in the mines. Those who can't, or *won't*, wind up homeless and starving.

"Yeah," one of them says lazily, the clanging of his boots growing louder as the men descend. "I nearly fell off the bridge today during that quake."

Lacy and I giggle. Drape has a reputation for tumbling off the sides of bridges during earthquakes. I swear, every other time there's a quake, the kid is crossing a mining bridge. I'm surprised he's alive. Drape pinches his lips together, and we try to contain our laughter.

The men continue their casual banter and eventually reach the base floor. I hold my breath as they head down the stretch of tunnel that will lead them back to the Slack. When they're out of sight, the three of us hurry out of our hiding spot and head up, treading lightly on the metallic stairs. At the top, we enter into a more elevated tunnel, scrap metal lined walls leading to a large doorway.

"You have the pass cards?" Lacy asks.

I nod and dig in my pocket. The pass cards are one of my prouder thefts. They allow me to gain access to just about anywhere, and it makes my side hobby of "borrowing" much easier. With a quick swipe down a panel by the entrance, the double doors *whoosh* back. The three of us scurry inside the immense, airy bay and hide behind a cluster of crates.

The shipping center is probably the cleanest, most soot free place in the mine. People actually sweep here, and even use cleaning products. It's almost hilarious, as if we're Leeches living on the surface. The ceiling, walls, and floor are different here, too. Not cobbled together out of scrap metal, and built to last.

"Check it," Lacy whispers, gesturing to the shafts and one of the Leeches.

"Whoa," Drape breathes. He's never seen a Leech, but their stiff, dark uniforms are a dead giveaway. They're also cleaner, and don't have that inevitable miner's cough. Lacy and I have gone on a few excursions without him, so we've seen them once or twice. Leeches rarely grace us with their presence unless there's been a shipping error or they're sending special gifts. I grin as I see several fellow dwellers pulling crate after crate from the elevator shafts.

"Oh, they must have something really valuable today," I say under my breath. "And whatever it is, they've got a lot of it. Good call coming today, Lacy. With that many crates, if one or two items go missing, it's unlikely they'll notice."

"Maybe it's extra rations?" Drape whispers, his voice full of innocent hope.

It's doubtful, but I don't want to ruin that smile of his. I glance away, not answering him, straining to hear what the Leeches are saying, but I can't quite make the conversation out. Their voices are even smoother than the guards, their lungs untainted by mining tunnels at all. Fresh air daily.

Mutant freaks, I think, though I know I only pretend to see these people as monsters to make myself feel better. To stay sane.

"Let's get closer," I whisper, raising my finger to my lips.

They both agree, and we cautiously rise to our feet, stepping high to avoid our slip-resistant boots skidding on and marking the shiny floor. Can't leave evidence. We work our way around the outer wall of the space, staying out of the Leeches' sight. Most of them have clearly never been below the earth, given how jumpy they are, and the guards are gushing all over them in an attempt to gain their favor.

Pathetic.

With us on the opposite side, we're hidden amongst the cluster of shipment arrivals. The Leeches and mining guards have congregated in the center of the room. The three of us stand behind one massive crate that towers high above our heads. The lid sits askew; this one has already been pried loose. Drape taps my shoulder and motions to a label on the face of the crate. *Yasay Tulbert* reads the stamp on the side. I've never been a fan of the mining boss, so the thought of stealing goods meant for him makes a thrill twitch in my stomach.

The Leeches jet for the elevators and soon they're gone. All but three of the guards quickly tail them out of the shipment area and toward the exit leading back into the Slack.

It's now or never.

"Lend me a boost?" I whisper. "Let's have a peek at what our slimy friends brought us."

Drape and Lacy grin back at me. They bend down low and extend their interlocked hands to one another. I place my right foot in Drape's palms, and my left I give to Lacy. Together, they boost me until I'm high enough to grip the edge of the crate. A shadow from the corner of the room casts over the half-empty crate, so I can't really tell what I'm seeing just yet.

I lean in, and then it happens. The crate creaks from the weight I put on it. The three remaining guards spin toward us. In an instant, I recognize one of them. His balding scalp gleams from the fluorescent glow above as he steps in our direction, a furious scowl on his face.

But he's no guard. It's Yasay.

Just our luck. I wish I had checked out the group of men a little better before attempting to rob them. My stomach churns as that large, balding cretin stumbles our way. Yasay isn't exactly known for being merciful.

Drape suddenly pushes up from underneath my right foot, tumbling me into the crate. My shoulder smacks into the wood and pain shoots down my arm. I bite down hard to stifle a cry.

"Do you hear that?" Yasay growls.

There's no hiding the fact we're here now. I shift to see what's going on through a crack in the crate's side.

Like a flash, Drape moves out in front of the men. That stupid, scrawny ginger is offering himself up as a sacrificial lamb to save mine and Lacy's hides. Why did he have to go and do that?

"Hey, Yasay," Drape says playfully.

"You're in trouble, boy!" Yasay calls as the two guards follow close behind him.

"Sorry… so sorry." Drape waves. "I didn't mean to be in here."

Lacy, giggling like a little girl, saunters out and curtains her arms around Drape, giving him a stern kiss on the cheek. I cross my arms over my chest, knowing what she has planned certainly won't work.

"Ooh, we got caught," Lacy says, as if this isn't a horrendous offense. She laughs and nuzzles her nose into Drape's collarbone, acting as though they were just two lovers caught in the act.

Yasay is *not* buying it. I don't have to see his expression to know that.

"Make sure no one else is in here!" Yasay

orders the guards in his croaking voice. He sneers and yanks Lacy away from Drape, pulling the two of them apart.

I move back, heart racing. What if the guards check the crate? In a flash, I tuck myself in a corner alongside the only metal container in the shipment. Unable to resist, I quietly open the box. If we make it out of here, I don't want to leave empty-handed.

Inside sits a tiny, black device. It's oval in shape, with a glass touch panel and a protruding tip. The metal container also has Yasay's name on it. What's so special about this one?

"I don't know what the big deal is," Lacy says. "You know how hard it is to get some privacy around here, Yasay. The door was left open, is all."

"It's *coded*! It doesn't get *left open*!" Yasay yells.

Ignoring them, I stare at the item. What could it be? I snatch it up just as Lacy releases a cry. I jump, almost dropping the device, and it beeps to life.

Oh crap. Any sound from this thing is bound to alert the guards. I stuff it in my pocket, pressing my hand over it as it emits three muffled beeps. The device vibrates and something pricks my wrist. I jolt back, bashing my skull against the side of the crate, and my head spins.

CHAPTER 2

I blink and my focus returns.

What happened?

A throbbing sensation coming from the back of my head brings me to my senses. On my hands and knees, I scurry to the corner of the crate. I peer out through the crack, catching a glimpse of Lacy, or at least her legs. A guard stands with a long stun weapon pointed at Drape.

Drape raises both hands up, stammering, "I-I-I..." He steps back, shaking. "Don't shock me," he pleads, but the man gets Drape right in his gut and he doubles over, landing next to Lacy.

Panic floods me. I know coming into the shipment area was stupid, but knocking out trespassers with that kind of weapon is an overreach of power. These are the only people I have in this world. I can't lose them.

My fingertips tingle and a warm sensation floods my body. I touch the device in my pocket and the memories flood back. I feel different. My vision whirls and an urge to sleep consumes me.

Breathe, Fin. Your friends need you.

Heart racing, I slowly rise. Instinctively, I flex my muscles. Every nerve ending pricks under my skin. My thoughts speed in a million different directions, but I'm also calm. My heart rate returns to normal, and a strange sense of peace and clarity overtakes me.

Yes, I'm *very* different.

I pull the device out of my pocket and flip it over. The letters GMK are printed on the back. Somehow, I decipher the acronym, like the answer was yanked from my memory. The device is a Genetic Mod Kit—a type of device used to manipulate the genetic structure of human beings and turn the elite into the privileged Enhanced Human Coalition.

Twenty minutes ago, if a person had asked me to explain exactly what an EHC was capable of, I doubt I'd have known. Now, it's as though my brain is a computer with an advanced search engine. All the data I've ever collected is back there, stored, and all I need to do is recall it.

EHCs... what *do* I know about them? There are always rumors flying around about advanced strength and stamina, enhanced intelligence, and that their cells can replicate quicker to help heal skin affected by radiation.

I work myself up out of the wooden crate, forming a plan to distract the guards. Silently, I land on bent knees, still hidden by the crate. I look around, but no one saw me. Near the edge of the crate opening juts a sharp nail. There's no rust, and they update us on tetanus anyway, so I suck in a breath and drag my finger across the metal, wincing. Blood flows from the wound, dripping down my hand. I let the blood drop to the floor in a tiny puddle.

Good. This will do.

Around the corner, Yasay's waving away the two guards, who are dragging the incredibly limp bodies of Lacy and Drape.

"Just bring them to the holding cell," Yasay orders, turning his back to me.

I dive between two smaller crates just as Yasay goes behind the one I've just left. A third guard joins him in his search. How in the world am I supposed to get around these two to go after Lacy and Drape?

The new guard grabs a step ladder for Yasay, who climbs into the crate. A moment later he lets out a string of profanities. He has to know the genetic mod kit is missing.

"Those kids are dead! *Dead*!" Yasay roars.

A guard bends to the floor to check out the little pool of my blood.

"Hey, Yasay," the guard says. "I found someth—"

With a swift kick under the ladder, I bounce it up in the air and catch it with both hands. I fling the base of the ladder into the guard's face and knock him out cold.

"What's taking you so long? Pass me down the ladder!" Yasay shouts.

I kneel and snatch the guard's pass card. A small part of me feels bad for Yasay. He's older, and I'm sure he'd worked his whole life in the miserable mines before becoming who he is now. The other part of me is just impressed his fat self was able to climb into the crate with the ladder to begin with, though not bad enough to help him, of course.

I make for the exit to find Lacy and Drape. Yasay said something about holding cells. As if my mind is a step ahead of me, I can perfectly envision the entire underground city. By simply analyzing everything I know, I'm able to deduce the exact location of these so-called holding cells. I pat my pocket for the device and curve down the tunnel, racing to my imprisoned friends.

I turn a corner down another deep tunnel with smooth walls, more like a fluorescently lit science lab than the rugged caves I'm used to. I hear voices and duck into a darker corridor.

"Where's Yasay?" a man asks, followed by the dull clunk of boots stomping by my hiding place. "He was supposed to meet me twenty minutes ago."

Stuck in that crate.

"Who knows?" the other man says. "Maybe

checking the latest shipments. He just sent those two kids down here from there."

The shadows from the men in the bright lights dance across the ceiling and soon it's quiet again. They're gone.

I grip the wall and notice the cut on my hand has nearly healed. It wasn't that deep, but it should still be bleeding.

I hurry for another door. It requires a pass card as well, so I swipe a different one from my small collection.

"*Access denied,*" it says.

"Unbelievable," I mutter.

Not giving up, I study the exit, forming a plan. A ledge sits just above it, and to my right is a stairwell leading up. I scurry up the metal stairs and throw myself over the edge, gripping the bottom of the ledge with my fingertips and the stairs with the tips of my boots. I wait.

An echoing mechanical voice sounds through the loudspeakers, but I can't make out the words because of the ringing in my ears from hanging upside down. I'm fairly certain the alarm is meant to alert the security staff, meaning Yasay's likely gotten out of his hole.

The doors slide open. As a man darts out, I release my feet from the stairwell and swoop down, landing square in front of the guard.

"Hey!" he yells, and I throw a violent kick into his kneecap.

Snap.

The man screams and falls to the ground. A pang of guilt shoots through my core until a description of a person sounding like me is blared via the alert system. The feeling vanishes and I race outside just before the door *whooshes* shut. The now-closed entrance muffles any cries of agony the man makes out in the hall.

Alert blaring, I one-eighty and do a mental scan of the room. A schematic forms in my mind. I visualize the three-story space and its exits from all angles, then bolt for the single area—under one of the ledges—in the enormous room where I can remain unspotted from all angles. Right beside me is a door with the words HOLDING CELLS etched into it.

Luck or destiny?

Four guards simultaneously appear from various doors—two on the second floor, one on the top, and the other on the base floor. As I calculated, no one can see me. Like a hawk, I watch the guard on the main level. He's the one most likely to spot me.

"Some girl stole Yasay's shipment?" one of the guards from above shouts down toward the man standing nearest to me. A simple twist of his head and he'll spot me.

"Yeah! You got a name yet?" the guard on the main level yells back. "I didn't hear the alarm. What's this tramp look like?"

"You didn't hear the alarm? Are you deaf?"

The guards above continue arguing. The one standing way too close for comfort rotates toward me, but I'm too fast for him. He barely does a double take before I fling a fist at him, nailing him in the throat. He gags and can't do much more since I twist him my way and wrap my arms tightly around him, choking him until he passes out. I ease him to the floor, out of view of the other men. Understanding the proper technique to overpower a guard like that was effortless, and having this new strength didn't hurt either.

"Sorry, but it's me or you," I mutter, not that he can hear me.

I swipe the security card off the unconscious guard and run it through the scanner. The door beeps quietly and I dart in.

"Hey! Over there!" one of the guards shouts.

The door *whooshes* closed behind me and I kick the control panel, shattering it. That should keep them out. I whip around and get right to work on locating my friends.

"This is just stupid! Why am I in a jail cell just for screwing up?" Lacy's patronizing voice echoes down the hall. "Haven't you ever been young once, buddy? I'll bet you were a lady killer in your prime!"

I wince. *Lacy, Lacy, Lacy… what will I do with you?* I dart down the hall.

"I swear, if you don't shut up, I'm gonna zap

your tiny—" The guard pauses and turns in my direction as I round the corner, scowling when he sees me. He's tall, well built, and much larger than me. I guess I should have waited before bolting around the corner, assessed the situation a bit.

"Fin?" Lacy's staring out from her cramped, windowless, cement prison, eyes like saucers. Drape bolts up from his seat and stands by Lacy.

Growling, the guard snags his radio and calls into it. "I found the brat the EHC is searching for—"

I leap at him and kick the radio out of his hands. With a *thud*, I land firmly on my feet. He scowls and lunges for me, reaching for my arm. I move back and grab his wrist. His eyes go wide as I pull him into his lunge. He trips, fumbling toward me. With my free hand, I throw a solid punch into his gut. The man exhales and gags while doubling over onto his knees. Still gripping his wrist, I fling a second punch into his jaw. He collapses, out cold.

Not sure if I really like my new self, but I could have used this skill for bullies back at the Oven.

Above, I get a clear view of my friends. Lacy's eyes are wide, but she's obviously quite impressed with my maneuver. Horror blankets Drape's whiter-than-usual complexion.

Lacy presses herself tighter against the bars. "What the—"

"Get back. We gotta go."

Without question, they obey. The bars are weak

and rusted, and after a quick analysis, I determine the lock is of poor design. Breathing deeply, I step back. Just two kicks and the lock on the heavy iron door cracks.

"Pull," I say.

Lacy and Drape walk forward, each grabbing the bars and giving a quick tug. The entire door shimmies free, clanging as they fumble to push it out of the way.

"Follow me." I rotate, racing from the room. The screech of electric saws sounds from the entrance with the busted panel. If there was an alternate door in here, the guards would have taken it to get to us instead of attempting to break down a perfectly good one.

There must *be at least two ways in.*

I dash the opposite way of the saws. We race down the corridor and stop when it comes to a dead end. I scan the space for an escape and find it. I point.

"There."

Lacy and Drape glance up to see an air shaft high above our heads.

"Um…" Drape mutters. "No way we're getting to that, Fin."

I ignore him. "Get ready to boost me."

Lacy and Drape give each other a confused look.

"You're wasting time. Just do it," I say.

The two wait across from one another in the

same manner they had earlier for the crate business. I step back to get a running start and both of them wince.

"Have some faith."

I run toward them and scurry from their palms to their shoulders. With a leap, I grab the gaping shaft and pull myself up and into the vent.

"Whoa! Nice!" Lacy exclaims as I reach down to them. Drape is shorter than Lacy, so he climbs up onto her shoulders. I yank him up.

"How'd you get so strong?" Drape asks, making his way past me in the cramped shaft.

I clutch his arm. "Hold on. I'm lowering you down to Lacy."

"Fin, I know I'm not the biggest guy and all, but there's no way you can pull us *both* up," he says.

I furrow my brow. "No, she'll climb up you."

"And you'll hold us both?" he asks.

A loud creaking sounds from the entrance. The guards have almost gotten in.

"We don't have time to practice. Get up there." I push the poor kid head first out of the shaft, gripping him by his knees and ankles.

"Don't drop me!" he yelps.

Lacy obeys me and climbs up him with ease. "Impressive."

"Get back," I hiss as the shaft starts to groan under our combined weight. Lacy scurries further back into the vent and I haul Drape up just as a clanking noise, followed by a huge *bang* of the door falling in, echoes our way.

"Come." I lead them through the air shaft on hands and knees. In my mind, I map out the vents. Our best bet is to head toward the Slack and get lost in the incoming and outgoing crowds of people.

Lacy and Drape stay close behind, putting an incredible amount of faith in me. Shouts resonate from beyond the shaft. At one of the vents, we spot loads of uniformed EHC members pouring into the space below. Dark and tactical in appearance, they dress for function and intimidation. It's always pretty serious when they bring in the EHC, so I'm positive our little jailbreak initiated an automated EHC alert. I can only imagine what they'll do to us if they catch us and then find out we have a stolen mod kit.

Finally, we get to the area we need to be, the middle of the Slack's tunnel systems.

"Stop," I whisper. "Time to disappear." I kick a vent cover down and round to them. "Listen up. Land on bent knees and tuck and roll. It's a long way down."

Not waiting for a response, I allow myself to fall. Not resisting the momentum, I tumble and roll. I pop back upright and look up at the ventilation shaft, waiting for my friends. They stare down at me, wide-eyed and not moving. Twenty or so onlookers around me gape at me as well. I suppose I *did* just fall ten feet from the vents. I'd hoped this area would have been more densely populated at this time, but no such luck.

"Hurry up!" I plead to my friends.

Lacy, the braver of the two, mimics my fall to the best of her abilities. She lands well, but tries to fight gravity and smacks her face into the rocky earth. She grunts as she stands up, hands instinctively reaching for her scraped cheek.

"You're fine," I say, a tad harsher than I meant to. Drape has his feet hanging out of the vent, but he's frozen. We probably shouldn't have left him for last. "Drape, right now!"

Shouts echo from the entryway of the tunnel. In the distance, men in black uniforms violently shove dwellers out of the way. EHC operatives, the big guns. Not good.

"Drape, fall!" I command, heart racing. No way I'm leaving that kid behind.

Somehow, the extra force in my voice compels him to do it. He lands in a heap, tumbling and shrieking. I shake my head and mentally cuss at him.

"My ankle!" he cries.

"Let's go, you big baby." I tug him to his feet and Lacy and I help him down deeper into the tunnel.

"There they are!" a male on the opposite side of the crowd bellows.

Drape is able to walk on his own, but he's struggling. The EHC operatives close in so fast I can practically feel them breathing down our necks. The complicated twists and turns of the Slack mixed with adrenaline and fear messes with my logic.

We skid to a halt.

Oh no.

"Dead end!" Lacy yells.

The EHC operatives' noise echoes behind us. As soon as they come around the corner, we're screwed.

"What are we going to do?" Drape cries. "Why did they call in the EHC?"

My brain races a million miles an hour as it attempts to calculate a way out of this. Endless ideas rise, but every scenario I run ends with us in body bags.

"They went this way, sir!" a distant voice shouts.

A creaking noise against the cave wall makes me whip around, breath hitching as a segment of rock appears to move, forming an escape.

"Hurry! Inside!" a soft voice calls.

CHAPTER 3

"This way," the tiny voice of our savior insists.

If it weren't for the small gas lantern the young girl is carrying, I wouldn't be able to see in front of my face. She spins to face us, walking backward, and raises the lamp in our direction. She's gorgeous, perhaps ten or eleven years old, and quite short and petite. The child has beautiful blonde hair and blue eyes, and though she's not smiling now, I'm certain if she were, it would be lovely.

"What *is* this place?" Drape whispers, his voice echoing.

"It was a Deep Earth subway system pre-Flip." The girl twists on her heels and walks forward again.

Deep Earth. All our mining equipment has a logo with that name on it, as do most of the buildings where I live.

"Who are you?" I've never seen her working in the mines before, but there are a lot of people I don't know.

"You first," she says. "And why was the EHC after you?"

She's just a kid. She's not a threat. "Finley A298. You can call me Fin."

"Drape G374," Drape's voice resonates from behind.

Lacy hesitates. "Lacy A292. Now who are *you*?"

"Cia. Cia Breslin."

No ID code? No wonder I don't know her. She must be one of the homeless who hide out in the Slack. The only people I know of without ID numbers are the mine bosses and the EHC. I've heard people who live in the Slack give themselves last names, kind of like the way the world was prior to the Flip. I scan the shadowy tunnel. This hidden subway system must be one of their little-known hiding spots.

"What a sweet name," I say.

We turn into another subway tunnel system, tracks intact.

"Now, why were EHC operatives chasing you?" Cia asks.

I open my mouth to answer when suddenly a boy appears, blocking the way. He grips what appears to be a plasma soldering torch—probably stolen from the miners. The homeless are even bigger thieves than *I* am. The torch seems to have been converted; a lengthy barrel like a rifle now attached to it. I don't intend to learn how it works.

"Cia, get back," the boy orders, switching the piece of machinery on. A slight glow emits from the tip of the barrel, ready to fire. The boy is tall, well-built, and handsome. Maybe near my age. By his blonde hair, worn slightly long, and those bright blue irises, I have no doubt that he's related to Cia.

And by his clenched jaw and dangerous scowl, I have no doubt he'll pull the trigger of that plasma torch if we so much as twitch.

"Sky!" Cia screeches, wedging herself between us and him, causing him to lower the weapon. "Don't do that."

Sky snags Cia by the waist and practically tosses her out of the way, keeping the weapon pointed in our direction.

"Make one move, and I'll kill you," he growls.

Intensity fills every contour of his face. Scavengers—the homeless—have been known to be quite desperate.

I throw my hands into the air, a plan worming its way into my mind. "We didn't mean to intrude."

"Cia, why did you bring miners in here?" he snaps at the young girl, now standing beside him.

"The EHC was chasing them, Sky," Cia says. "They were in trouble."

"*EHC*?" Sky whips back to us, fury brewing in his eyes. "Did they see you?"

"I—I don't think so," she cries.

"You three need to leave. *Now*," he says to us.

Lacy steps toward him. "If we go, the ops will

kill us." Her voice quavers slightly, like when the bullies from the Oven used to corner us.

Sky whips up the gun. "If you don't leave, *I'm* going to kill you."

"*Listen*," I order. Sky curls his lip in protest, but it doesn't stop me. "If we go, we'll wind up leading the EHC operatives right here. They'll see us, then they'll find you and drag you both to the mines, and I suspect you wouldn't like that very much. We need to work *together*."

Sky glares at me, but he lowers the barrel of his weapon. "Why are they chasing you?"

"We got busted snooping through new shipments," Lacy says.

"They wouldn't send EHC operatives after common thieves," Sky argues. "That's a job for tunnel guards."

"They must think we stole something important or saw something we shouldn't have," Drape reasons. "But we weren't there long enough to see crap. They freaked out. We just need a place to lay low for a while."

Guilt rips through my stomach as I touch the device in my pocket, but I push the feeling away. There's nothing I can do about having it now.

Sky hesitates, but lowers his weapon completely. "Fine," he snarls, and marches us down the dark subway tunnel.

Lacy breaks the silence. "So, do you two live in these tunnels back here?"

"Yes, so that we can avoid people. People like *you*," Sky answers with an angry huff.

"So you don't work in the mines then?"

"Nope," Cia says.

"Then why don't you all live in the Slack with the rest of the homeless? I can't imagine living in this dark tunnel is any fun."

"It's not about *fun*," Sky snaps. "It's about staying alive with my sister."

I cut Lacy off from her questions. "If they stayed in the Slack, eventually the tunnel guards or EHC ops would raid the homeless and force these two into the mines."

"Well, at least then they wouldn't have to be scavengers," Lacy whispers to me, but I'm certain Sky heard her.

"Sky and Cia are in two very different age brackets. They'd be separated."

"I'd rather be separated from my brother or sister than us both having to live like *this*," Lacy admits.

Being from the Oven, there's not much understanding of kinship. You know whoever is in your graduating class, like Lacy and me. Drape was several classes behind us, and he's pretty much the only one from his group that we know. For all I know, Drape could be my brother. That would make things real odd between us given how he feels, but, luckily, he looks nothing like me. Dwellers don't have the privilege of family unless they manage to beat the system, as Sky and Cia seem to have done, and that normally comes at a cost.

Sky shoots Lacy a filthy glare. "I'd rather live *this* way than be a slave to the Leeches like *you*."

Lacy presses her fists on her hips. "I'm not a slave."

"Keep telling yourself that," he says. "How old were you when they put you to work?"

Lacy frowns. "Eight."

"The Oven cooked you slowly then," Sky says. "I've seen kids as young as six being drug to the mines." He leads us to the right. "Here we are."

Oil lanterns and various lighting sources sit and hang all around, but a likely stolen generator and a string of lanterns keep the area well lit. A reinforced hole in the subway tunnel's wall appears to be where they sleep. Truthfully, it's more spacious than the community dorms. They have two makeshift beds, a tiny cooking area, and various luxuries they've probably pilfered throughout the years. Compared to our home, this is almost like a paradise, if only because of the immense privacy they obviously enjoy. I've seen a few homeless families scurry out of sight in the tunnels over the years and always wondered how they made it.

"I know where each one of my meals comes from," Lacy says, hanging onto the conversation.

Sky grins. "That's true. But *I* don't have food

held back for not completing my quota. Have you ever been hungry just because someone stole your rations? Not me. We grow our food. It's been years since we've gone hungry. In fact, we rarely have to scavenge anymore. We trade the extra food we grow for supplies. I bet even you couldn't say that you don't have to steal to get by, Ms. Privilege."

Lacy crosses her arms, defeated for now.

Sky certainly has a point. This sort of freedom seems rather tempting, even if it means living in a dark tunnel with no one but your sister. As he and Lacy were arguing, I didn't notice that Cia had wandered off. She's skipping back to us now, carrying a plate of what I guess are berries, not that I've seen real ones before.

"Hungry?" she chirps in our direction, then gestures to seats made of small crates.

I smile at her and we all sit. I stare at the unusual, large, red berry. I pinch the green leaves on the top, hold it to my nose, and sniff. It's the most delicious scent I've ever experienced. Sweet and fruity. Both Lacy and Drape study the berries as well.

Sky laughs. "You three have never had strawberries, have you?"

I've *heard* of strawberries, but I certainly haven't *had* one. I pop it in my mouth, squishing the incredibly sweet, tart fruit between my tongue and the roof of my mouth. Yes, it seems there *are* advantages to not working in the mines, a surprising new discovery for me. The majority of the scavengers I've seen are either starving to death, being beaten by guards, or having their bodies removed from public places. Sky has clearly worked very hard to provide for his sister.

"Where did you get strawberries?" Drape asks as he greedily grabs a second from the plate.

"My uncle found seeds and started growing them down here when he was my age. It took a lot of effort on his part, and a bit of stolen equipment to get it working, but we have a garden. He taught me how to man it," Sky explains, wearing a constant scowl.

Cia hops up from her seat. "I'm gonna get them water from the well."

"No," Sky practically growls. "You don't even know these people, and you're giving them our food *and* water!"

She laughs in her older brother's face. "You and I both know we have plenty of water. Don't be so mean, Sky." She skips off, happy as can be.

"Where is your uncle now?" Lacy asks.

"Dead."

Screech!

Metal clangs, and I twist to find Drape fiddling with a pile of junk beside him.

Sky jumps to his feet. "Don't touch my stuff! Keep your hands where I can see them!" he roars, cheeks bright red, clutching his weapon to let us know he's tempted to draw it out again.

Drape winces and folds his hands in his lap, avoiding eye contact with Sky. "Sorry. I was just looking."

"Sure you were." Sky settles back down.

I rise from my seat and Sky eyes me.

"Where are *you* headed?" he asks.

"Just doing a perimeter search to confirm we weren't tracked, if that's okay with you." I spin on my heel and walk out of their sight. Once I am, I slip my hand into my pocket and pull out the GMK.

"Stay until my sister gets back with the water," I hear Sky say to Drape and Lacy. "But then you need to go."

A low whistle sounds and I stuff the device back in my pocket. I turn to find everyone on their feet, Sky with his gun readied.

"Impressive set up here."

Stepping into the light of the room is a tall, slender man dressed in fine, black clothing. He places his hands on his hips and peers around, his narrow, dark eyes scanning the details of Sky and Cia's home. His handsome figure and perfect jawline is no doubt evidence of his breeding as a member of the EHC, and, by his uniform, he's an elite operative.

"Now, let's see here…" he nearly sings. "We have one, two… yes, *two* escaped prisoners. A miner who, no doubt, had to do with their escape, and… a scavenger. All hiding out together. How quaint."

"They came here. I had nothing to do with whatever trouble they're in," Sky says, keeping his distance. He lowers his weapon and sets it on the table.

Nice. Real classy.

Although I can't say *I* wouldn't opt to save my skin over that of a stranger's.

"I'll be the judge of that," the operative says. "You four are coming with me."

We freeze. Not one good thing will come from us following the operative.

The man tips his head with a *tsk*. "Apparently you need a little help."

He smiles and jerks his right thumb over his shoulder toward the darkness outside the room. A glow appears as one of his fellow operatives flips on a portable electric lamp. Half a dozen armed men, dressed in similar uniforms as their ringleader, flank him. Between two towering guards is Cia—shaking, bound, her face wet with tears, her mouth covered by one of the men's meaty palms.

My muscles tense. Everything in me wants to race to her.

"Cia!" Sky's voice shakes with anger.

"You damn leech!" I bark at the lead operative and lunge at him, my fists clenched.

He laughs and swings at me. I shorten my stride, causing his fist to fly past me and allowing me to surprise him with a quick, fierce punch to his shoulder, my knuckles cracking at the blow. He flings his foot into my stomach and sends me flying back. Pain sears through me, but I straighten and ready myself for another attack. His jaw clenches as he grips his injured shoulder. My strength and swiftness, while not to the level of his own, caught him off guard.

"You're a slag!" he says, eying my miner's clothes. "How?"

"Hey, Nero, don't let that little girl one-up you!" one of his men teases from a few yards behind him.

I keep my distance, but remain in a fighting stance. This time, though, I plan to be extra cautious. This man is trained, where I am not.

"Fin?" Lacy's voice echoes. I can hear her shock.

I have a feeling this standoff is about to get much more violent. Possibly deadly. Drape, Lacy, Sky, Cia—none of this is their fault.

I should never have stolen the mod kit.

I need to fix my mistake.

"Nero Kyoto, stand down and release the child."

The sound of his full name causes him to raise his eyebrows. I point a single finger to the left of my chest and the man, Nero, instinctively checks to see his own last name etched into his operative's uniform.

"Arrest her!" Nero orders, pointing at me.

His men scramble to obey. A loud *zap* whips by my ear. I instinctively cover both ears and shriek. The blue burst zips past Nero and me, barely missing him to strike down one of the operatives and sends him back into a column. His singed body slides down to the ground. The stream of hot plasma rips into the cement pillar before the discharge fades out.

"You idiot!" Sky yells at Drape, who's clutching Sky's homemade weapon. The entire room rumbles and shudders violently as the support beam disintegrates and the ceiling begins to cave in.

"Get back!" Nero orders his men.

Enormous rocks and slabs of cement from the old subway tunnel rain down into the room.

"Cia!" Sky calls.

Lacy and I grab him to keep him from darting under the rapidly falling debris.

"No, other way!" I order.

The lights flicker as I force Sky back into Lacy and Drape, and the four of us dart down the tunnel in the opposite direction of the EHC operatives. Just as the last of Sky's home is buried in rubble, I catch Nero throwing Cia over his shoulder and sprinting away, just barely saving her from the back end of an old subway car as it falls through from the tunnel above us, completely cutting us off from our enemy.

Silt and dust fill our nostrils and we all begin to cough and choke. "This way," Sky wheezes, and we follow after him.

He slips into a crack in the foundation. We rush to funnel into the opening, knocking into one another. We can't all fit at once. I usher Lacy and Drape to go ahead of me. They nod and Lacy leads with Drape close behind. Once they're clear, I squeeze through and fall deep into a ditch just as more rock and cracked cement come crashing down, tumbling on top of the others in a heap.

CHAPTER 4

My elbow smashes into Lacy's jaw. At least I *think* it's her jaw. And I'm pretty sure one of the boys' heads is rammed into my lower back.

"Get off me," I mumble at whoever will listen.

About three feet above us is the crack in the subway tunnel's foundation. Thick dust pours out, raining down on us.

"Anyone got a light?" Lacy asks.

A few seconds go by before one of us makes a fumbling noise followed by a *crack*, lighting the space a glowing green.

Lacy points to the glowing plastic in Sky's hand. "What's that?"

"It's a glow stick. I always carry a couple," Sky growls, gasping for air. His eyes are wild and his entire upper body is tense. "I'm gonna kill you." He lunges and pushes out of our heap. Lacy grunts and mumbles curses under her breath. "Where are you, you little *punk*?" Sky waves the glow stick in front of us and reaches down, coming back up with the scruff of Drape's shirt in his hand. He jerks the shocked kid, Drape's forehead covered in blood.

"Stop it!" Lacy snatches at Sky, but he shoves her down and manages to pull Drape into a headlock, dropping his glow stick.

"This is *your* fault!" Sky roars. "They took my sister because of *you*!"

"Help!" Drape cries, trying desperately to squirm out of Sky's clutches. Drape is feisty and breaks himself free, but Sky manages to get in two blows before Drape gets enough distance from him. I leap forward and wedge myself between them.

"Enough!"

I grab Sky by his throat and kick Drape back. Sky gags and poor Drape falls face-first once again. Drape whines as Lacy, now holding the glow stick, helps him up. I pin Sky's back against a cemented wall, gripping his throat with one hand and his right arm with the other. Sky's eyes flare open in surprise.

"Be still," I command.

Sky exhales and his shoulders relax. I release his throat and he gasps, keeling forward when I let go.

"We need to get as far from here as we can before they start searching for us again," Lacy insists.

We give Sky a moment to regain his breath. "I'm sorry," Drape whispers to him, offering a hand. I know the kid means it. He wouldn't hurt a fly if he didn't have to.

Sky growls and slaps him away, pushing himself up.

"I didn't mean to cause that collapse. I was trying to protect Fin," Drape adds, his voice shaking. Sky doesn't respond.

"Fin doesn't need you to protect her, Drape," Lacy says. She turns my way, and I can just barely make out her figure in the dim light. "You don't need *any* protection, right, Fin? You took out a man twice your size at the holding cell *and* flung Drape and Sky around as if they were children. I mean, you've always been strong when you protected Drape and me when we were little, but *this* is new."

"It's a bad time for this," I say, wanting her to be quiet.

"You could have snapped my neck just then. That's not normal for a Dweller," Sky adds, rubbing his throat. He digs into his pocket to produce a second glow stick, cracks it, and gives it a shake. The stick provides us with a dash of extra illumination, and all three of them stare at me, waiting for answers.

I rake my hands through my hair, uncomfortable. "While I was in that crate in the shipping zone, I came across this." I reach into my cargo pants and pull out the device. "I must have hit a button or something because it... it changed me."

"Changed you how?" Lacy asks.

"I feel different. Stronger. Maybe quicker, too."

"It sounds like you've been modified," Sky says.

"What!" Lacy exclaims with more excitement than she did the day she was gifted extra rations for locating a collection of gold in her tunnel. "Fin, that's amazing! Do me next!"

"*What*? *No*!" Drape yells. "Are you insane? You don't know what sorts of side effects that thing has. She's a *dweller*!" He stares at me, terrified.

I shove the device back in my pocket. "Don't be ridiculous, Lacy. I'm not going to modify you—not until we know if that's even what this thing did."

Sky steps back and begins to pace. "You three are nothing but trouble. Cia should never have saved you." He rubs at the back of his neck. "What are they going to do to her? They'll force her into the mines..." He stops pacing and peers into the dark tunnel behind us. "Okay, where are we... the old sewage system... which way back?"

"*Sewage* system?" Drape whispers in disgust.

Lacy looks back at me. "What are we going to do?"

This was my fault, and I can't throw that kid to the fire. Cia was kind to us, and it got her in trouble. We invaded their home, and Drape caused the cave in.

"I have an idea, if you're willing to listen. If

you break into mining security, you could use the camera systems to locate your sister."

"I don't know the mines…" Sky says. "I've spent my whole life avoiding them. You have to help me."

I angle to Lacy and Drape. Drape seems uncertain, but doesn't reveal what he's thinking. Lacy shakes her head in a firm *no*.

"Take me there!" Sky shouts. "You have to! This is your fault! All of this is your fault!"

He's right. This *is* all our fault.

"We'll take you to the mine's security room," I say.

Lacy moans, but doesn't argue. Most the time she acts like she doesn't, but I know she has a heart.

"But only if you help us find our way out of this sewage tunnel," I add for insurance.

"Fine. Let's go," Sky says.

We follow him further into the darkness. The dim light from Sky's glow things guide our path. While these systems haven't been used for probably more than a hundred years, they still hold the reek of sulfur that makes my eyes water.

"I think the bleeding has stopped," Drape says, wiping his forehead with his shirt. No one says anything back, but I'm relieved to hear the news.

Lacy sneaks up beside me and leans in. "Let me get another peek at that mod kit. You know I'm an expert at black market stuff like that."

"No." Lacy's my best friend, but it doesn't mean I trust her.

"Come on, Finley. You know I've always been curious about Yasay's not-so-secret operations. Maybe I can figure out how they smuggled illegal tech down here."

Lacy curiously forces her fingers into my pocket. I slap her hand away, giving her a firm glare.

"Just let me *see* it," she insists. "Do you think Yasay paid someone to steal it? I bet people would give him whatever they could to be modified."

"I don't know," I whisper. "You can see it later. Not now." I nod up ahead to Drape, who's attempting to make small talk with Sky. "He's upset. Now's not the time for games, okay? You can play black market detective later."

"Fine," she says. "Do you really *feel* different?"

"Yeah, I guess. The biggest change is my mind, though. I'm... processing differently," I say, but it's difficult to explain.

"Processing differently? What do you mean?"

"It's like... like Ms. Kayla from the Oven. Remember how she and that oaf Lorie would play chess in their downtime? They would brag about how they could plan so many moves ahead. That's kind of how I feel. Like I'm just... thinking. Constantly. Just thinking. Observing. Predicting. Without even trying."

"Weird," she says.

∞

"Guys, we're here." Drape points upward.

We exited the sewage system a good way back and re-entered the subway tunnel far from the place Nero's goons had likely exited. Gazing up, there's an entryway to an old, vertical mining shaft. I cringe at how narrow it is.

"We'll be able to climb up this and exit down Abandoned Tunnel 238," Drape says. "That one is blocked off, but something tells me Fin can handle some flimsy particle board."

"Yeah," I say, confident that I can.

"Good, because Tunnel 238 is connected to that new air shaft right outside the mining security office."

"How do you know?" Lacy asks him.

"Remember last year when I broke my right wrist during that cave in?"

"Yeah?"

"They had me on light duty for a couple months. I worked on installing the air vents."

"Installing air vents is *light* duty?" Sky mutters, shaking his head.

"Ready to climb?" I ask the group as I step up underneath the entrance of the dark, seemingly never-ending shaft. "Drape, lead the way."

Drape nods, and Lacy and I give him a lift with our palms to raise him up into the shaft. He moans in pain, but doesn't complain. His ankle must still be a bit tender, but it's not slowing him down. Lacy tosses her glow stick up to Drape, and he hangs it around his neck.

"You next," I say to Lacy.

Sky moves to stand by me, helping me lift her up in a similar way as Drape.

"Now you," I say to Sky.

All the bravado he had before has vanished and worry fills his face. "I'm not trained for this."

"I'll help you up, and Lacy should be able to pull you the rest of the way. After we get there, you'll need to help me."

"Okay," he says.

I bend down and put out my palm. This is surprisingly easy—lifting him up on my own. Sky pulls me up into the shaft and I grasp on tight to the wooden beams that make up the bottom of the wall as the others begin the long ascension.

This particular shaft is squared, and there are plenty of wooden boards to grab onto. The further Drape and Lacy get from us, the darker it gets at our end of the shaft. Sky's singular glow stick dangles from his neck. He shouldn't, but he's constantly checking below. His face is covered in a layer of sweat from the climb. We get a few more yards and then a board snaps under his right foot. His hands slip, and I grip the boards around me, pressing my boots into the shaft wall and bracing myself for a tight impact.

I glance up, imagining the worst, but he's gripped firmly to some boards and is working to secure his footing.

"You got this!" I call to him, and after a moment of gasping and much struggle, his feet manage to find a home on a sturdier board. "All right, you're fine." I climb toward him. "Sky?" I beckon as I reach him. I can hear his quick inhales, but I can't squeeze past him. "*Sky*," I say firmly, but he's not responding.

"Everything all right down there?" Lacy's voice echoes. "We found the tunnel."

No wonder it had gotten so dark. Lacy and Drape and their glow stick were no longer in the shaft with us at all.

"Yes, we're fine! Give us a minute!" I call up to her, then, whispering to Sky, "Keep moving."

He still doesn't respond.

"Sky, listen to me. You're not used to this sort of climbing. Your arms and legs are bound to give out, and you'll send both of us falling. We've climbed nearly twenty feet now. We're almost there. I'm right behind you, all right? I promise I won't let you fall."

He takes in a deep breath. "Okay, okay. I just needed a minute."

Sky moves, and the glow stick on his neck loosens. I try to grab it as it falls past me, but miss, leaving the two of us in utter darkness in the middle of a creaky old mining shaft vent.

"You guys alright?" Lacy calls again.

"Everything's fine! We just lost our light!" I call back, trying to make it sound like a minor inconvenience.

"I can't see," Sky says, stating the obvious. "It's pitch black."

"You'll have to feel around."

"I can't," he says at last. "I can't do this."

"Yes, you can. We're almost there." I reach upward and locate a steady board for him with my hand, then stretch back and touch his right calf. "Let me guide your footing."

Slowly—*painfully* slowly—I help him reposition his feet.

"You'll have to locate a place to grab on with your hands. I can't do that for you," I say.

"I know," he grumbles, taking his time. "I got this."

Finally. Truthfully, I was worried, but he starts moving faster than I expected. As we make our way upwards, a tiny bit of green illumination appears above our heads.

"About time." Lacy pulls Sky up into the abandoned tunnel.

I climb up myself, and, thanks to the higher ceilings, stretch out my back. This abandoned tunnel is massive, clearly mined dry of any minerals the EHC could possibly want.

"Sky did a great job," I say. "Didn't you Sky?"

He looks at me and nods. The anger he had

toward us earlier is gone. "Thanks to you."

"The shaft we need isn't far," Drape says. A dim light trickles in from the floor of the tunnel where sloppy miners broke through to the corridor below. Beneath us is a walkway in the Slack.

"Geez, Drape, you look awful. Hold on." I pull a cloth from my cargo shorts. "Here, wipe your face better."

"Thanks," Drape says as he cleans the dried blood from his cheek.

Sky steps forward. "Can we get moving, now? I need to find Cia."

"Of course." Drape hands me the now-bloodied cloth. I shove it back into my pocket and we hurry down the tunnel, allowing Drape up front. It doesn't take long for him to point out a ventilation shaft, moving aside to let Lacy and I yank its cover out of the wall of the tunnel. Drape dives in first, but I go in behind him, followed by Sky and then Lacy. The shaft slopes downward, so we slide on our bellies to prevent ourselves from tumbling forward. Compared to the mining shaft, the air ventilation system is cool against my skin.

Drape halts. "We're here," he whispers, pointing to a vent cover. "I don't think anyone is down this hall right now, but just past the corner there's probably a bunch of tunnel guards outside the security room."

"We need to come up with a distraction," Lacy whispers.

"There are normally only two guards in front of the main entrance of security," I say. "If we can knock them out and use a key card to get inside the back lobby, there should be a seismometer set up in the room. All it would take is a decent shake to set that equipment off."

"Seismometer?" Sky echoes.

"It detects earthquakes," Drape explains. "They're stationed in the most active areas. The earthquake alarm will sound and everyone will rush into emergency mode. We can sneak into the main security room with no problem and lock ourselves in."

"There's an alternate ventilation shaft in there we can use to escape and find wherever they've taken Cia," I say. "So, first things first. We need to overpower the guards."

"Can you do that yourself?" Drape asks.

"I'm strong, but I'm not stupid. I'll need backup, guys."

I kick the vent cover out and it makes a loud *clank* when it hits the metal flooring below. I cling above the exit as two guards rush to investigate the noise. Good, just two. With a look to my friends, I allow myself to fall. I land hard right on top of one guard and the two of us tumble down together.

"What the—" the second guard shrieks as Drape and Sky tumble down from the vents, just barely managing not to fall on one another.

The guard I landed on is out cold. Lacy comes

next and the remaining tunnel guard charges at her. The poor guy is no match for the four of us. Drape, Sky, and Lacy all grab hold of him, and I bean him in the back of the head with a tightly wadded fist. He falls in a heap.

"All right, let's move," I say.

I snatch the man's keycard and we make our way to the security wing, a stone fortress not far from us. The cemented brick surrounding the security wing stretches out of our line of sight, wrapping around the bend.

I turn and raise my finger to my lips. With a quick swipe of the keycard and *peep* from the lock, we open the door and enter an extended hallway with metallic flooring and cemented brick walls and ceiling.

"Any idea about the location of the main control?" Lacy asks.

"All the way at the end," I reply, but I'm only half sure.

The hallway juts to the right and I pause to peer around the corner, giving an all clear signal. We walk into the hallway, which extends into a sky bridge overlooking an enormous room full of security personnel. This won't be as easy as I thought.

"If we walk across that bridge, we'll be spotted," Lacy says.

"Yeah, but see what's on the other side?" I point toward the end of the stretch at a door prominently labeled *Security Headquarters*. "I'm guessing that's main control."

"If they see us go in, we'll trap ourselves inside with guards just waiting on us," Drape protests.

I shake my head. "No. Remember? We can use the air vent in the main control."

"I only installed a few vents," Drape argues. "I don't know if I'll be able to get us where we need to go!"

"You're going to have to," I tell him. "Get ready. Hopefully this key card will get us in there."

There's a collective deep breath, and then we bolt. We step out from the hall and onto the sky bridge, making ourselves quite visible to the guards below.

"Hey!" I hear a man shout from beneath us. A group of guards rush to side rooms that will take them up to this level.

At the door, I slide the keycard.

Beep.

"Lock us in," I instruct as we slip inside.

Lacy rips a fire extinguisher from the wall and bashes in the key card scanner.

"What are you *doing*?" sounds a nearby cry. A man jumps from his seat behind an abundant display of computer screens. He charges at us and I aim a kick into his gut. As he falls, I strike his head with my knee. He's out.

"Ouch," Drape says, wincing.

Muffled shouts sound just outside the door.

"Hurry, the seismograph!" I yell, pointing at the equipment set up in the corner. "Set it off before these goons have a chance to call for backup."

Drape and Sky both dash for the machine. "How?" Sky asks.

"Like this!" Drape violently kicks the table the machine is seated on. Almost immediately, a screechy alarm sounds off. Pain rips through my eardrums. We throw our hands up to block out the sound. On the security screens above, masses of hysterical people are shown running throughout the main operations cavern and tunnels, trying to get to safe zones.

"Good," I say. "Do that every once in a while so the alarm doesn't stop." I find the enormous keyboard laid out in front of the monitors and reason my way around it. In a flash, I'm able to figure out exactly how this equipment works.

Lacy stands beside me, peering over my shoulder in awe. "How do you know how to use that?" Computer skills were not exactly taught to us in the Oven. I've maybe used one on a handful of occasions. We were bred to be miners, and that was all.

"I just had to figure it out," I say, and shortly after I pull up various camera angles throughout the shafts and in other areas in the mines. "There," I say when I spot a smug Nero Kyoto walking alongside Cia, his hand roughly gripping her elbow.

"Found her," I growl, and Sky is suddenly beside me, practically breathing down my neck.

"Where is she?" he demands. "What mining tunnel?"

I frown as the realization hits me. "They're not entering a mining tunnel."

"Well *where* then?" Sky snaps.

"They're headed to the surface transport level."

"What! Why?"

I have to change cameras a couple times to keep up with Nero and his thugs, and we watch in horror as Cia is forced onto a transport tram that will escort her to the surface world. It's possible for dwellers like Cia to be transported to the surface inside of sealed capsules to prevent radiation poisoning, but even within those capsules, dwellers will die given time and exposure.

"I'm going after her," I insist. "I'm going to the surface."

CHAPTER 5

Boom.

Sounds of popping metal echoes as the guards bust the door down. We scurry up into the air vents and away from our pursuers, the earthquake alarm still blaring. Beyond the confines of our cramped shaft, I hear people screaming and yelling

I lead, Drape right behind me, the two of us attempting to guide the others through the maze of ventilation shafts.

"I think this vent will lead us to the back of the Slack," Drape says, grunting slightly as he crawls behind me.

"We should be able to reach the transport levels on foot," I add. "Everyone will be heading into the barracks, thanks to the alarms."

We drop down out of the vent and into an empty hall near the transport level. There's not a single guard to be seen, but there's not much reason to have this area heavily secured. No dweller would be stupid enough to try to make their way up to the surface and risk being exposed to the radiation.

I point to a stairwell. "The railway and elevator systems are just up there."

Racing up several levels of stairs, my ears pop. Must be the change in air pressure. The sensation increases the nervousness spinning in my stomach as we near the surface, and by the tense expressions on everyone's faces, I can only assume they're feeling the same.

At the top of the stairs, we enter an enormous cavern at least a thousand feet wide, and over three times that in height. The transportation station.

"Whoa," Lacy murmurs.

It's like we're standing in a giant pit. Up the tall, circular cavern, there's no end in sight. The darkness conceals anything more than a few hundred feet up. Its natural opening has long been sealed to limit the influx of radiation. It's now just an access point for the EHC. Carved and welded into the rocky walls, railway lines, as well as elevator shafts, stretch up as far as we can see.

"So how are we supposed to get into one of the pods and all the way up to the surface?" Sky asks.

"This is not a *we* thing. I'm rescuing Cia alone. No way I'm putting you all in more danger," I reply, grabbing a standard-issue miner's water bladder that hangs near the entrance we came from. "You three stay down here where you won't risk radiation poisoning."

"Or you could stop being a martyr trying to go it alone," Lacy says, her cheeks reddened. "Modify me and I can go, too!"

"No!" I shout. "You don't know what sort of risks are associated with—"

"Lacy is right, Fin," Drape interjects. "You're gonna need help."

"You two shut up!" Sky barks. "This is *my* sister you're talking about. If anyone is going with her, it'll be me."

"So a random street kid we don't know gets to be modified while we stay here?" Lacy mutters to Drape.

Sky glares at her. "Yeah, because *I'm* not motivated by some sort of weird, greedy desire to be turned into a Leech."

"I'm not *greedy*," Lacy hisses. "I just don't want to be taken advantage of anymore. There are a lot of crappy people back there." She holds back tears as she points back in the direction of the Slack. "People are the worst. You and Drape are all I need."

She's right. When Lacy was five, several of the older kids decided to pick on her because she was small. Most of the Oven workers turned a blind eye, but not me. I took plenty of punches in my time while standing up for her, but it was worth it. We did the same thing for Drape.

I pop Sky in the arm so he returns his attention to me instead of verbally attacking my friends.

"Listen, Sky, I know you want to save her, but you'll die up there."

"Not if you modify me!" he argues.

"I'm lucky I wasn't killed. I don't even know how to work this piece of equipment." I throw the full water pack over my shoulder and reach down to retrieve the mod kit. A part of me longs to smash it here and now, but as I fiddle my fingers in my pocket, I realize it's gone. I spin on my heel. "Lacy!"

My friend, the most fearless pick-pocket I've ever known, has managed to one-up me.

I pounce as she desperately presses a few buttons. Before I can snatch it from her, a bolt of energy cracks out of the device, and the shock shuts her down as she drops. I fall in a heap at her side.

"Lacy!" I shout in unison with Drape. The three of us circle her. She's sprawled out, her limbs spread in different directions.

"You all right?" Drape asks nervously, bending down beside her.

Lacy blinks slowly in an attempt to gather her senses. "I'm okay," she breathes.

Drape and I each grab an arm, sitting her up. We help her stand and I snatch the device up from the ground, gripping it tightly and considering smashing it.

I swing my attention from the black device back to Lacy. "That was really stupid. What were you thinking?"

"I feel a little woozy… whoa…" Her eyes roll back in her head somewhat, then snap back. "I feel different."

Concern overtakes my anger. "Different how? Different bad?"

"Stronger," she growls, yanking her arms away from us.

The fury at her impulsiveness returns as my fist forms into a tight ball. "Let's see about that!" I bellow and punch her in the gut.

She doubles over, but her recovery speed is impressive. Lacy rises and holds up her fists. "Why did you do that?"

"You could have *killed* yourself!" I screech.

"Quiet!" Sky shouts and then points.

Far up the cavern wall, one of the trams moves upward. Although, there are no people here in the cavern itself, there are people visible through the windows of the interior-lit trams.

Lacy gives me a haughty look, raising her eyebrows. "Sorry, but I wasn't going to let you be the only hero."

"This isn't about being a hero," I snarl. "This is about *thinking*. Thinking *clearly*, which you're not doing, are you?"

"I'm thinking just fine," Lacy says.

"You said you felt different. Different *how*?"

"I told you. Stronger, I guess."

"But that's it?"

She pauses, then frowns intently. "Hey, I got gypped! You got smarter, right?"

"Keep it down," Drape hisses. "You're lucky it didn't *kill* you, Lacy."

"Now modify me," Sky says, tapping my shoulder.

I spin and glare at him. "What? No."

"You think I'm planning on trusting you and this brainless slag to get my sister back?" Sky snarls, waving a hand in Lacy's direction.

Lacy's jaw drops and her fists clench. "What did you just call me?"

Dwellers don't call us miners "*slags*". It's an insult only the EHC uses.

Sky ignores Lacy, his attention trained on me. "I get there are risks, but it's my *sister*. Please."

"You don't know how dangerous that thing might be," Drape warns.

Sky's eyes narrow, and he rounds toward Drape, anger brewing. "I'm going. Whether I'm modified or not."

"That's ridiculous!" I yell. "You'll die."

In my distraction, Lacy snatches the device right out of my hand. She tosses it to Sky.

"Don't!" I cry.

Another shockwave bursts out of the device, sending Sky back into the cavern wall with a *crack*. He falls forward, dropping the device and landing on his hands and knees.

"Oh, man... I'm gonna be sick," he mumbles.

"Look who's brainless now. Get up," I growl, yanking him to his feet. Slowly blinking, his face goes white.

"Let go." He snaps out of it, examining his hands and flexing his fingers. The blood returns to his cheeks.

Drape steps our way. "Do you... do you feel alright?"

Sky smiles. "I do. Stronger."

"*Just* stronger?" Lacy asks.

He pauses for a beat. "Yeah."

"No enhanced cognitive abilities either?" I ask, and he shakes his head. I cross my arms and swing toward Lacy. "Why would you do that? It's one thing to put yourself in danger, but *this*? You could have killed him."

"We're three for three," Lacy says. "So far your little theory about this tech being dangerous is starting to seem far-fetched. Maybe you're not so smart after all."

"There's no time for this. Let's go," Sky says. "How do we get up the cavern? If we try to board one of those trams, we're bound to get busted by guards."

I stare up into the abyss. He's right. What's done is done, and I can have it out with Lacy later. "We climb."

"Whoa!" Lacy shoots back. "We can't free climb that. You can't even see the top."

I flex my arms. It would be a serious climb, but I'm experienced. Above us wait various ledges. It's not like Sky and I couldn't take an occasional break on them. I ignore Lacy. She'll start to notice her strength in greater bursts soon, and she'll realize how possible this is for us now.

"Sky, are you ready?" I ask.

He exhales deeply. "Yeah."

"Okay, I'm going, too," Lacy pipes in.

"No way," I start to argue.

"You two aren't leaving by yourselves." She rolls her eyes and turns to Drape. "You go back to the Slack. Hide out. Hopefully none of the guards will recognize you and you'll be able to just slip back in."

"Oh, yeah, sure, Lacy," Drape replies sarcastically. "The pasty red-head isn't going to be the one who gets recognized, right?" He bends down and picks up the device.

"Drape, don't!" I yell, wishing I had snatched the tech back after Sky had used it.

"Three for three, right?" he says.

He presses the buttons and his knees buckle. He topples over onto his back Moaning, he slowly starts to sit up.

"Drape, you feel all right?" Lacy asks, but Drape doesn't answer. He falls back, convulsing.

"Drape!" I rush to his side. His eyes roll into the back of his head and he makes a horrible gurgling sound. His entire body twitches violently as I grab for him. "Drape, can you hear me?"

Lacy screams, a whaling sound of horror mixed with a stuttered breath.

"What do I do?" I can figure out how to deal with a broken limb, but not seizures.

Drape goes limp in my arms and Lacy throws herself beside him. "Drape?" she sobs.

Emotions I've never felt swirl in my mind. He's like family to me. This isn't right.

A few seconds pass and Drape coughs, his eyelids shooting wide open.

"You idiot!" I say, wrapping my arms around his neck.

He sits upright and gazes into my eyes. "Are you an angel?"

"What?" I yelp.

But before he has a chance to answer, Drape clutches his midsection. "I might be sick."

Lacy leans down and punches him in the arm. "Don't scare us like that!"

Drape shakes his head, the tiny bit of color he has returning to his face, and jumps up to his feet, apparently forgetting his stomach. "Wow, this is incredible!"

"Let me guess, you're not suddenly a smarty-pants like Fin, right?" Lacy asks.

"Um, maybe? How would I even know?" Drape asks.

"Trust me, you'd know," I say. "But you can't come with us. Not after that."

Drape opens his mouth to argue when the blare of an oncoming transport train rattles the rails above.

"That transport stops on the interior of this cavern," Sky says. "We have to move. Now!"

I curse under my breath and Drape crosses his arms and smiles triumphantly. He won't have time to make it back to the Slack before the oncoming assortment of EHC operatives arrives. "We need to make it to that next ledge before they get off the tram, or they'll see us."

The four of us make for the side of the dim cavern. It's beyond intimidating, but we need to go.

"You got any extra glow sticks?" I ask Sky.

"No," he says.

"Sorry. I dropped mine back there in the vents, too," Drape pipes in.

I grasp the nearest handhold I can and pull myself up with hardly any effort. The rest tail right behind me. With his new strength, Sky is actually doing a fair job of climbing now, but he's slow.

"Hurry up," I whisper. "The tram just slid into the station."

We all pick up the pace, and Drape reaches the ledge before us. *Well, that's a first.* The ledge is narrow, so the four of us squish together to stay out of sight from the EHC operatives exiting the tram.

They're too far down to hear what they're saying, but their voices are low and full of anger. Searching for us, I suppose. I grin. If these men knew just how close we were, fifteen feet over their heads, watching them. The last of the ops head down a tunnel, out of sight.

"You see that ledge up there?" I point. "That's our next stop."

"That has to be a forty-foot climb," Drape says.

"Maybe you should just stay here, Drape," I insist. "Wait it out. There could be more side effects. Can you even climb further with your messed up ankle?"

"My ankle's fine now. I feel great. I'm not going to sit here on this ledge waiting around just to wind up getting caught by EHC," he argues. "I can do it."

"You and Sky aren't exactly climbers," Lacy adds.

"I climbed that shaft just fine!" Drape argues.

"It wasn't meant as an insult, *Dope*!" Lacy says, play punching him. "I just mean that Fin and I should partner up with each of you. Show you the rocks to grip and where to place your footing."

"Oh," Drape says.

"All right." I stand up on the ledge and start to climb. "Sky, match me. Put your left foot here, not here." I show him where I'm placing my boot.

And so we begin our climb. It's not easy. Even with my new strength, it takes us twice the time to make it to the nearest ledge. By the time we get there, my lungs burn and all I want to do is rest, but from the scene around us, my wishes are dashed.

"This is a track," I say. "We can't rest here. We might get hit by a shuttle train."

Drape puts his hands on his knees, panting. "Great," he moans.

I grab for the rock face again and the rest follow. It's fifty feet or so to the next ledge. When we reach it, all four of us are drenched in sweat. I even feel a greater tickle of surface heat and radiation on my skin with every few yards we advance. Pressure stings my ears again from the elevation change. Nausea roils in my stomach. I gulp to keep it down, but it only accentuates my parched tongue. One after another, we all suck water from the tubing that sticks out from my water bladder. The water is warm and not quite as refreshing as I hoped it would be, but good enough.

At the sixth ledge, the jutting edges of the rocky cavern allow even less light than there was lower down. We have a considerable distance to climb, and I don't know if we can do this, but I force myself to continue moving. The rest continue to follow my lead, Sky right on my heals. His bond with his sister is different than what I feel for Lacy and Drape. There's something more there—something deeper driving him. Something buried in me longs to understand it.

We haven't stopped for at least thirty minutes now. Exhaustion and the lack of visibility overwhelm me and I visualize myself just letting go. Giving up. My lids sink shut when a red glow pierces through the endless darkness. I open my eyes to the source above our heads, slightly illuminating the next ledge.

Hope flows into my core like a jolt of energy. "We're almost there!"

I pull myself up onto the closest ledge, followed by my friends. Relief floods my body. This ledge is considerably larger than the others. We collapse and lean with our backs to the cavern wall, stretching our legs out in front of us.

"What's that light?" Drape asks, breathless from the climb.

"I think… it might be the Sun," I pant.

The hair on my arms stands on end at the thought. The Sun. It's like a mythical creature I've just learned is real. I wonder what it's like. What awaits us at the top of this cavern? What awaits us on the surface?

"It's sealed up there. How can it be the sun?" Lacy asks.

"I don't know, but I can feel the warmth. It's different."

"Whatever it is, that's a long way away," Drape says. "You guys, I really need to pause for a minute. I can't keep up."

I let out a sigh of relief that someone finally said it. We've got at least an additional thousand feet to climb, and there's no way we'll make it without resting for a bit. Free-climbing is dangerous enough inside the mining tunnels, but this is entirely different. If we fall, we wouldn't just be dead, we'd be *mush*.

We finish off the rest of the water and I toss the empty pack to the side. The air hits my sweat-slicked back and feels wonderful. We sit in silence for who knows how long and I study the walls. There are no more ledges I can see apart from tracks, and resting there would be dangerous.

"Hey Fin," Lacy whispers, distracting me from my analysis. "Something is different. I feel off."

I look past her and see the boys creeping over the edge, amazed at the drop.

"I told you that device isn't safe. You should've listened to me."

She shrugs. "Oh, there was no way you could've stopped me from using it, Fin. I'm not letting you do this alone. I'm just going to have to deal with it."

Sky sits back up and turns to me. "Are we going to do this or what?"

I flick my attention back to Lacy, who's now staring up the rock face. I sure hope she can deal with it. I'm worried for her, but we'll have to continue our talk later. We need to move.

"Get ready," I say at length. My existence as a common dweller is one ledge from changing forever. "We'll have to climb the rest in one go."

How we do it, I'm not sure. Sheer will, I guess, but one by one we make it up. Arms shaking and back throbbing, I wrench myself onto the top of the cavern. The ache from the blisters on my fingers eases a bit, but blood still slicks my hands.

My relief is short-lived as a wave of heat envelops me. I pull myself to my feet and there it is. Bright rays of light stream just ahead of us, burning my eyes with their intensity. I reach for the light as if it's calling to me. It's a sort of side shaft that opens to the surface, a natural escape that bypasses the EHC controlled exit. It's a break we definitely need.

There's no changing our minds now.

CHAPTER 6

We emerge from the dark into a scene none of us have ever witnessed. We've heard stories about it. The underground EHC personnel would often brag about it to make us feel even worse about our lives, but I never knew it was like this.

A hazy blue horizon stretches as far as my imagination can ponder. Resting below, a cracked and rusty landscape contrasts the beauty above. I've only seen vegetation in books, and the dry, brittle shrubs that dot the flat surface don't live up to the vibrant life I've read about. While hot and dry, the air smells fresh, lacking the minerals and dust we inhale every day.

"I thought... since we were... modified... this wouldn't be... so bad," Lacy gasps, kneeling down on the desert-like terrain.

"We've spent... our entire... lives... underground," I pant. "We need time... to acclimate."

"Ahrg," Drape mutters. "Don't stare... directly... at the sun."

Slowly, my vision starts to adjust. A massive cement hatch covers the opening of the cavern. Several shafts jut out from the top. They must be where the trains exit and enter. Next to the underground seal is a sizable building that was likely the entry station to the underground. There's not much to it. Just random structures and pieces of equipment on the roofs.

We manage to sneak over to what I guess is tall shrubbery and hide in the brush. There's nothing but train tracks leading out of the station in all directions for as far as we can see.

Even under the scattered shade, the sunlight burns my skin. I keep my head between my bent knees to block out a portion of the brightness.

"It's beautiful," Lacy says after a few minutes.

"What is?" I ask, not looking.

"The sky. That's what it's called, right?"

"Yes," Sky answers. "I should know, it's my namesake."

I squint at Lacy, blinking to clear my blurred vision. Her head is tipped back, gazing upward. I glance up and find she's right. The sun is low, and there's white and purplish puffy artwork spread out above our heads for miles and miles.

The scene breaks when a large, flying piece of machinery whips by, clearly heading somewhere in a hurry.

"What was that?" Drape shouts excitedly, and I throw my hand out to cover his mouth.

"A hovercraft, maybe," I whisper, pulling my hand back. "Get down."

The four of us crouch in the scrub and watch. The ship lands right outside the station on the pavement. I've heard the EHC ops—who *grace* us with their presence below—talk about these machines that glide through the air. A hatch opens and people unload and load various crates of whatever the miners have gathered for the EHCs for the day.

"We need to go to that station," Sky says. "That's where Nero took Cia, right?"

"No way. Not now," I say. "We'll be spotted."

Sky tenses and rakes away a sweaty clump of blond hair from his forehead. "Then when?"

I rack my brain for information. The sun rises and falls. It's low in the sky now. Eventually, it will vanish.

"In a few hours, I think the sun will set, making it dark. Plus, we're all weak and need rest before we try some crazy rescue attempt. Sure, we're enhanced now, but I assume everyone else we'll be dealing with up here is, too."

Sky scoffs, but relents. He knows I'm right. We sit in silence under the shadow of the vegetation. A considerable amount of time passes, then Lacy stands up and stretches.

"I've got to say, I love how quickly I'm bouncing back. If I had tried a climb like that yesterday, I would be flat on my back for days. Even you were pretty impressive, Sky. I bet you haven't scaled a rock wall in your life, right?"

"Never," he says.

"Ok, I'm curious now. What's it like, Sky?" Lacy asks.

"What's *what* like?"

"Your life. I mean, almost every dweller works the mines. We were taught that we're the lucky ones, you know? But you... you're different. What's it like?"

I turn my attention to Sky, quite curious myself. He raises his arms above his head, stretching out his shoulders. In the light, this is probably the best view I've gotten of him all day. I try not to bother myself with boys—nothing but trouble—but his clear blue eyes fascinate me. Or it could be delirium from the heat.

"To me, you three are just slaves to the people who live on the surface. I may be poor and occasionally steal for supplies, but at least I'm free."

Lacy frowns, but doesn't take the bait. "How did this even happen for you anyway? Were your parents homeless, too, so they just kept you there?"

"No," Sky says. "My mom was an infant caregiver in the orphanage. She had tiny pregnancies, which helped her keep them a secret.

She had help from a few of the workers. She'd always wear baggy clothes to hide her pregnancy with Cia, and did the same with me. They kept me smuggled in the staff quarters at the orphanage."

Sky's mother wanted him so badly she hid him?

"So you *were* at the Oven?" Drape asks.

"For a while. But I never left my mother's quarters. Not once. When I was seven, right after Cia was born, my mother came in one night, shoved her in my arms, and a man who was her brother ushered us to the Slack. Pretty sure she realized she couldn't hide us forever." Sadness washes over his face. "That was the last time I saw my mother."

My chest tightens, both aching for him and with a twinge of jealousy. I didn't know my mother, but it doesn't mean I've never had dreams. "Your sister didn't know her?"

"No," Sky says. "But that doesn't stop her from making up silly stories. Cia has… an impressive imagination. I try not to talk about our mother to her, but she's insistent."

"How come you didn't search for your mom?" Drape asks, throwing pebbles at nearby vegetation.

"Before my uncle died, he would warn us of the EHC and how horrible life was as a miner. I guess I just accepted my existence."

He's right. Being free for your entire life just to be tossed into the mining labor force would be a death sentence. I turn to him and watch him tug on his shaggy bangs. There's an innocence to him, even after having to grow up fast and be a father figure to Cia.

"How'd your uncle die?" I ask.

Sky looks away and draws in a breath. "He trusted the wrong Dweller."

His words take me aback.

"He was running some supplies and a Dweller woman he knew ratted him out. I didn't know anything since I stayed confined mostly to our hiding place. Days later, one of his friends told me the EHC shot him."

"I'm so sorry we got you into this," I tell him. "We'll find her."

"I have hope. I do," he says, resting his head back. "I just don't know what life will be like after we do."

"It's going to be amazing," Lacy blurts out. "We're modified now, and we'll modify Cia, too. No more mines or hiding in dingy tunnels."

"You're *not* touching my sister," Sky insists. "I'll decide what's right for my family."

"I didn't mean anything by it," Lacy huffs. "We're not dwellers anymore… more like *gods*, now."

"You're kidding right?" I ask.

Lacy lets out a nervous laugh. "Oh, sure. But I kinda do feel like one." She sits back down, a satisfied smile stretching her lips, and stares out at the horizon. She's different since the modification.

It's like her sense of reality has been altered, as if the enhancement has affected her thoughts.

The sun settles further into the horizon and casts streaks of dark pink and purple across the sky. It's lovely, but I try not to let myself get distracted. That's not why we're here. Apparently I've started to get used to the radiation; my skin no longer burns or tickles from the exposure.

"It's time," I say. "We can try to sneak into the transport hub. Maybe we'll see Cia there, but if we don't, we can at least we can figure out what Nero did with her."

An alarm blares from the hub, making me jump.

"What's that for?" Drape squeaks.

"I don't know. Let's get closer," I say.

We dart to the outer wall of the station and squat down to stay out of sight. I inch up and peer around the corner. It's chaos, and the air is thick with stress. The EHC operatives scatter in all directions.

"No one goes in or out, you understand?" a distant voice calls to the panicky operatives.

I duck back behind the wall to my patiently waiting friends. "They're restricting access to the underground."

No one says anything. The weight of the device in my pocket presses against my leg. It doesn't require a modified mind to figure out what it is they're looking for, especially after my enhanced encounter with Nero.

"If they're sniffing for us, there's no way we can sneak into the station and just go walking around," Drape says.

Sky scoffs. Drape's right, but I suspect Sky has likely cast all concerns for safety aside.

I creep up to get a better view as a long, sleek shuttle train pulls into the hub, but it can't descend while the underground is blocked off. A handful of passengers exit, and a slender man with dark hair and a black uniform greets them,

"Nero," I say, and in a flash Sky practically climbs over me trying to get a peek.

"Where's Cia?" Sky whispers urgently, peeking over the edge of the wall.

I scan the passengers again, but don't find a child. "She's not with him."

"Where is she?" Sky asks, struggling to stay down.

Looking back at the train, it becomes clear. My new gift helps me analyze the situation.

Four tracks. All but this one has their trains stationed and shutdown. No crew, no lights—nothing. There's never more than one transport delivery at any one time. It only took us a couple hours to climb. A lead operative like Nero wouldn't leave his post in a crisis, but he *would* want his bargaining chip secure, and getting it far away would make the most sense.

"Wherever they came from," I say, pointing at the people scurrying about.

"Then we need to board that shuttle and take a ride," Sky growls between gritted teeth.

CHAPTER 7

I wait for the passengers to clear and then wave my friends forward. We bolt to the shuttle at the far end of the station. One of its sides is still opened to the station itself while the other looks out onto the seemingly endless desert terrain. Our only hope is that there's a way on board through that side.

We zigzag between railways and the pearly white, blue-striped shuttle glides into view. The sleek, clean exterior isn't like anything I've ever seen down below. Ahead lays our salvation: a doorway on the desert side. Unfortunately, the smooth door has no apparent manual handle.

"How do we open it?" Lacy asks.

Just as she speaks, the door *whooshes* back. A railway worker steps out and throws something to the ground. We duck out of his sight, and my breath hitches as he moves to close the door again, but Sky sneaks up behind the man, wraps his arm around his throat, and yanks the man back. The worker struggles for a moment, but quickly goes limp in Sky's arms. Sky drops him.

"You killed him!" Drape shrieks, coming out from our hiding spot.

I grab for Drape and snap my hand over his mouth. His eyes go wide. I shush him, then release him.

"No, I only made him pass out," Sky says. "I've done it before."

Drape bends down and checks. He sighs with relief. "He's breathing."

"I told you. Now let's get moving," Sky says.

"Hold on," I whisper. "People are bound to see this guy." I search the terrain and find what I'm looking for. "We'll hide him in the brush across the way."

Sky and I seize the worker and drag him to the brush. I feel sorry for the guy. He's just some poor sap who was in the wrong place at the wrong time. We dump him and rush back to the shuttle.

"*Last minute boarding*," sounds an unseen voice in the air.

We race up the four tiny stairs into the shuttle, and once we're all inside, Lacy quickly shuts the door. The space is packed with small crates, and a door separates this car from the rest of the shuttle.

I dash to the little glass window just taller than eye height on the door. Just beyond our reach, the car is filled with puffy red seats and wooden tables. Four passengers sit eating massive plates of food.

Just the sight causes my stomach to rumble. I haven't eaten since earlier today. I shake my head at the thought that the EHC can't even get from one location to the other without expecting to be treated like royalty.

"It's a passenger shuttle," I relay to the others. "Only a couple of people in there." I don't tell them about the food.

"I doubt there are too many passengers on board then," Lacy says. "This station is in the middle of nowhere."

"Probably ops," I reason. "Otherwise they wouldn't have much business coming out this way to the underground entrance to our sector."

I stretch up to the window again and a muffled voice from the intercom sounds through the glass. I have no clue what it's saying.

"Check it out!"

I turn. Lacy's digging in one of the small crates.

"No way, Lacy," I snap. "If they notice stuff missing, we'll get caught!"

She ignores me and keeps digging. "Look at all the goodies! Oh, *no way*!" A huge grin lights up her face and she produces a box. "Candy? It's chocolate!"

"What's chocolate?" I ask. The boys seem just as confused as me.

"I've had this once," she says. "One of the headmasters gave me a bite of his stash. He said he got it from an op who owed him a favor."

"What *is* it?" I ask again.

"*What is it?*" she echoes skeptically. "Only the most *amazing* food that has ever touched my lips!"

Lacy tears into the box and pulls out a handful of wrapped packages. She tosses each of us one and we rip open the wrappers to reveal a lumpy brown bar.

I frown. "Lacy, it looks like something you'd find in the men's latrine. I'm not eating this."

"Try it, trust me. And besides, we haven't eaten in hours, and we need to refuel after—"

The shuttle jolts, nearly knocking Lacy off her feet, but she's all smiles as she bites into the brown bar.

"We need to refuel from that climb," she finishes in a mumble, her mouth full.

The boys exchange tentative glances, and Drape raises his bar up to his nose and sniffs. He smiles and practically shoves the whole bar in his mouth. Sky apparently confirms that as a good sign and does the same.

After all we've experienced today, it's silly to worry about this, so I sniff the bar. A rich aroma fills my nose and I nibble the end. Creamy sweetness and a hint of rich bitterness floods over my taste buds. The flavor reminds me of coffee, which I've had a few times, but overly sweet coffee.

"So, this is what leeches eat, huh?"

I gulp down the rest of the bar just as Lacy is opening another for herself. She tosses me a second.

"It's so sweet. I can feel the sugar rotting my teeth as we speak," I say.

Going down, the candy turns my stomach slightly, but even so, I stuff the second chocolate bar into one of my pockets for safe keeping.

"What else is in there?" I ask, joining Lacy at the crate.

"I just want these," Drape mumbles, his mouth full of chocolate.

I stare at Lacy for bit as she licks her fingers clean of the treat. A warmth floods over me. I'm not sure I could be doing this without her.

"So," I whisper to Lacy, "have you ever wanted to find your parents?"

Lacy breaks off another chunk of the chocolate and stuffs it into her mouth. "No… why?" she asks, mouth full.

I shrug. "I don't know. Sky's story got me thinking. At least he *knows* who his mother and sister are. Family's really important to him. Look at how badly he wants Cia back. She's everything to him."

We dig into several of the crates. Half the food we find I've never even heard of, but I don't really care because *everything* I try is the most amazing thing I've ever tasted. I especially like the Turner's Turkey Jerky—sweet and savory all at once—but

I'm incredibility thankful for the boxes of juice that fill one of the containers.

I practically lose myself in the cuisine of the surface world when another jolt of the train sends me back into reality. I rise and take a peek out the window. Walking down the center of the aisle, a uniformed worker heads straight for us. Luckily, he's not paying me any attention.

"Someone's coming! Hide!" I gasp.

"What?" Drape leaps up in a panic. "There's nowhere *to* hide!"

He's right. The crates are far too small to use for cover. I whip around. My brain assesses the problem at lightning speed. "Can you three hold on tight?"

"What? What do you mean?" Lacy asks, her voice tense.

I don't answer and race to the exit door, throwing it open. "Hold. On. Tight."

Lacy gives me an unsure frown, but the three of them flood out of the shuttle, gripping the ledge surrounding the window outside. The wind roars past us. Who knows how fast we're going. It's not a safe speed for that kind of risk.

I close the door on their horrified faces, trying not to envision what could happen if they fall. Inside, I scale the interior wall, gripping the side of the doorway with a hand and foot and stretching my opposing limbs against the opposite wall. The door slides back, and I'm out of sight just in time as the railway worker enters.

"Roger!" he calls. The door shuts behind him. "Idiot…" He glances sourly around the shuttle, lips pinched together.

My arms and legs singe with pain as I push tighter into the corner.

"I swear, if that moron got left at the station…" He twists, and his eyes grow wide.

He sees me. It's not the best hiding spot, I know, but one of us had to stay inside the shuttle to reopen the door.

"Hey," I say and drop down.

"You're that missing dweller!" he gasps.

I dart the way of the exit door, knocking the man back with my shoulder as I pass him. Kicking the lock, it rattles open. The door flies back and wind gushes in. My group stumbles back into the car, each with a *thunk*.

"What the…?" The man regains his footing as he darts for Sky, who easily side-steps him. Both Lacy and I charge the man and knock him clear out the door. The man rolls uncontrollably when he hits the ground, dust billowing up around him. A wash of guilt floods my mind at what we just did to him, but the wind whips my hair into my face and refocuses me. I step back and slam the door shut.

I hurry back to the window, peering into the next car over. "People are leaving this shuttle and heading forward."

On the opposite end of the passenger car, I spot a touch panel. Maybe I can access information we can use.

I wait for the passengers to clear, then throw back the door. We race into the empty car. Ours was for storage, but this one is meant to be a luxurious experience for its passengers. Large windows line either side of the car. A beautiful view of the dimly lit desert terrain slides past. Above me, I search for the source of the illumination. A small but bright white circle rests high in the dark sky.

The moon. I've read about it, but seeing it in person is different. It's amazing how it seems to move with us, almost watching us.

"Wow!" Lacy plops down in one of the red, velvety chairs and leans back. "Ooh, it even reclines."

I shake my head at her childishness, but she never got a childhood. None of us did. So why not let her have one for a minute.

"What's in the next one?" Sky gestures to the door that leads into the next car up.

I hurry over and peer in. "That one's empty, too. We must be getting close to the tram's destination since all the passenger's decided to move up."

"What *is* its destination?" Drape asks.

I go to the touch panel. "I don't know, but let's see if we can find out."

I tap on the screen and it lights up. I play with the options for a bit and locate the schedule.

"Seems like we're heading to a city called Reso... It's an outpost in the New Delta Sector."

"Reso? I heard a leech mention that once," Lacy says.

The display panel has a search option, so I decide to do a little digging on the location we're about to enter. I frown at the information. "Great. It's an EHC Training Academy City."

"What's that mean?" Sky asks.

"It means they send the rich kids there to be brainwashed into making sure they know their position," Lacy explains. "The leeches constantly talk this place up like it's an exclusive boys' club."

"Sounds *great*," Sky says. "But what about my sister? That computer say anything about her?"

"Let me see what I can find." My fingers effortlessly navigate the display as if I've done this a thousand times. It's all just logic, though. Directory structures and search commands. I'm able to predict how these systems function.

"Ah, there she is!" I say. "There's a transport manifest. She was on this train on its last trip back to the underground station. Her final destination is marked as classified, though."

A low hum vibrates the panel, snapping me out of my lock on the system.

"*Passengers, please prepare for entry into Reso,*" an unseen voice echoes through the intercoms over our heads.

From out the window, a metropolis rapidly approaches in the distance. Even though it seems fairly small, it gives off a lot of brightness. The EHC would brag about their massive, wondrous cities on the surface—huge standing buildings that would block out the sun—but I'm pretty sure this isn't one of them. I guess the EHC could've exaggerated.

We pass an entire field of dark panels that reflect the moonlight. I can't recall what they are, but there's a lot of them. Beyond this, the full scope of the city reveals itself. Tethered, giant, hovering disks pour light down onto every inch of it. I've gotten so used to living in near darkness that the brightness amazes me. Tan and off-white buildings fill the skyline. Only sporadic trees and shrubbery provide any contrasting color.

"There's a ton of EHC out there," Sky says nervously, looking out the window.

My heart jolts. "Get back to the storage car. We have to jump."

We run back and stuff our pockets full with chocolate and jerky. I press the panel and the door slides back.

"Oh, this is gonna hurt," Drape mutters.

"Tuck and roll," I say, and dive out.

My body crashes to the earth and I land on bent knees, allowing myself to fall, tucking my arms and legs. Pain rushes in places I didn't even know I had, and I tumble overtop of myself several times. I scramble to my feet and wheel around to find my friends. Everyone is mostly unharmed. The shuttle rushes ahead and eventually stops at the station a good distance away.

"We're too visible," I say.

The air is stifling, thick, even without the sun, and our boots tend to sink into the loose earth, making our trek doubly hard. Even so, we make it into the city in a few minutes and duck into a dark alley between two buildings. Metal ladders run the entire way up the face of the building, and a generous ledge with a railing extends outside each window.

"We need a better view." I jog to the starting rung of the ladder and start to climb. My friends follow close behind. We reach the roof of the building and from here we can get a good look at what living on the surface is like. We have to be thirty yards up.

"Wow, would you check that out!" Drape says, inching toward the ledge.

Several crafts go zipping through the air between buildings nearly as high up as we are.

"I never knew flying cars were an actual thing! Cars pre-Flip didn't look like that."

Lacy lays a hand on his shoulder. "How do you know?"

"An old timer told me."

Lacy shrugs.

The light pouring out of the hovering streetlights brightens the streets below while keeping our roof concealed in darkness. I study the people walking up and down the street. Their clothes are all perfectly clean, wrinkle-free, and colorful, the style far from that of the cargo pants and stained tank tops I'm used to.

"First things first," I say. "We need to find different clothes." I watch my friends in amusement as they all examine what they're wearing.

"What's wrong with our clothes?" Sky asks.

"You look like a dweller, that's what. Especially Drape, Lacy, and me. We're covered in dirt, and Drape's shirt has pit stains."

Drape instinctively covers his armpits with his hands.

"Okay, so where are we going to get clothes?" Sky asks.

"Funny question coming from a scavenger," Lacy says. "We *steal* them."

With that, she joins me at my side and scans over the scene. I know what she's doing. She's scoping it out.

"What do you think?" I ask.

She doesn't answer for a few seconds, then points. "There."

I trace the direction of her hand and see a hover car, if that's what you call it, parked in an alley between two enormous buildings. The building to the left catches my attention. It's frightfully tall and narrow. It twists up, curving at the edges.

"What's in there?" I ask.

"I don't know, but we're gonna find out," Lacy says with a smile.

"It seems like it just arrived at the station... There might be luggage with clothes inside. Nice, Lacy."

One problem. To get there, we have to cross the street—a street that is filled with people, including EHC operatives, all heading home at the end of a long day.

"Well," I say. "This should be fun."

CHAPTER 8

We climb down the ladder to the alleyway. Across the street, the hovercar waits, but there are pedestrians all over.

"This will never work," Sky says.

"We stand out like coal among diamonds," Drape agrees.

"Really, Drape?" I say, smacking his shoulder.

"What?" He shrugs. "We do."

He's right. The thought that we could make it to the hovercar unnoticed, even at night, is one of delusion. I wait patiently, studying the crowd from the safety of the dark alley. In the distance, an even larger group makes its way toward us.

"Well, well," I murmur.

There's fifteen or so in the group, and they're dressed much more casually. Though they still appear very little like us, they're all drenched in sweat, and some wear baggier clothes. The women wear tight bras and sleek pants. The entire crowd jogs alongside one another, their eyes focused on the sidewalk in front of them.

"Feel like a quick jog?" I ask, crouching slightly as the runners approach. "Now."

The four of us bolt from the alley and take up the rear of the pack, amazingly unnoticed. They lead us right to the other side of the street past the parked hover car. We split from the group, keeping our casual, steady pace to avoid drawing attention. It works, and we make it to the alleyway near the car without so much as a glance from the people on the street.

Once it's clear, we dart to the side of the car facing the alley. An overhanging structure provides us with a bit of privacy from the main street.

I scan the vehicle, assessing the best way in. There's a handprint scanner on the door—not that it does us any good.

Lacy doesn't waste time. She walks up to the craft, looks around, and raises her elbow into the air, bringing it down to bash in the back window. My mouth drops and I hunch over, waiting for some sort of alarm to ring out, but nothing comes. Straightening up, I turn and cringe at the sight of such a lovely piece of machinery broken. It's a sleek, shiny vehicle, long in length and incredibly narrow. Lacy rummages around in the back and pulls out a few pieces of clothing.

"Aww, sweet, there *are* clothes," Lacy says with excitement. "Someone did their laundry just so we could have pretty, fresh outfits!"

She tosses me a pair of blue pants that seem to be close to my size. I go and hide behind the car and empty my pockets of the food we stole. Dropping my cargo pants, I wiggle into the new, tight, *"borrowed"* bottoms. "Got a shirt for me?" I ask.

"Hold on, I'm looking." Lacy tosses the boys a couple pairs of slim, black trousers.

"Why do they wear stuff like this?" Sky asks as he yanks them on. "It's hardly functional. They're tight and uncomfortable."

"I'm pretty sure their clothes aren't meant for comfort," I say. "They don't have to dig in the mines all day long."

Lacy tosses me a black shirt. I sigh and duck down to remove my working shirt. In the mines, we never change with the guys. The bosses don't want us getting any *ideas*. Not that I *want* any ideas. Having babies outside of the Oven's assigned schedule is not something I have any interest in. I know what it means if the underground population can't handle any more pregnancies.

I flick up my gaze and ignore Drape's roving eyes. No time for embarrassment now. As fast as I can, I pull on the form-fitting top and yank up the neckline—if you can *call* it a neckline since it seems nearer to my belly button than my neck compared to what I'm used to. I give up. It is what it is.

"Okay, everyone dressed?" I ask, snatching up my chocolate and jerky from the ground and stepping out from the back of the car.

Lacy's ready, dressed in similar attire as me.

"Whoa," Lacy gasps, gawking my way. "Dang, Fin."

Heat rushes up my cheeks as Sky and Drape stare in my direction. Drape smiles from ear to ear. "Wow."

Sky quickly turns away, his cheeks reddening.

"Stop it. We don't have time for this." I yank up the top as far as it will go and point to an emblem on my chest. "We're dressed like escort guards."

"Escort guards?" Drape asks, his smile falling away.

"You know, like bodyguards," Lacy clarifies.

"You see a bag or anything in there?' I ask.

Lacy peers into the vehicle and pulls out a satchel. I walk to her and take it from her hand.

"Everybody put your food in here for later," I say, adding my supplies to the bag. "We have no idea when our next meal will come, so we might need to ration."

Sky and Drape both shoot me sheepish looks.

"Uh…" Drape mumbles, "I already ate mine."

"When?" I huff.

He shrugs. "I donno. Maybe on the roof?"

I look to Sky. He only turns his body and looks away.

"Do *you* have any left, Lacy?"

She produces her own stash of chocolate and jerky and hands them to me. "Yeah, but only because it made my stomach hurt." She glares at Drape and Sky. "But I'm not sharing with these two pigs later."

"Stop!" a man's voice echoes through the alley.

I nearly drop the bag as my heart leaps. A man and a woman with pistols pointed our way strut toward us. My first instinct is to bolt, but I don't want to get shot. They're dressed similarly as we are, but their clothes appear closer to uniforms, and the woman's isn't so low cut.

"Whoa, what's the problem?" Lacy asks casually, playing off whatever the guards believe they just saw.

"The problem?" the woman sneers. "We just saw you stealing from the back of that hover car!"

"What? No." Lacy gestures to the vehicle. "This is mine. I lost my key card and had to bust in the back window."

They're not buying it. I could have told Lacy they wouldn't, but I guess she didn't realize the car has a handprint scanner. They don't use key cards like we do in the technically-neglected underground.

"Lacy…" I grumble, releasing the bag and raising my hands up. My mind gets to work formulating an escape.

"Hands up, right now!" the man shouts.

Everyone obeys, but my friends are giving me the eye, pleading for me to make a move. It's like they just don't get it. Sure, I'm modified now, but so is everyone else up here.

I scan the alley behind our attackers, but I'm coming up dry for a plan. Sweat trickles down my right cheek, but I don't dare move to wipe it away. This might be the end of the road.

"Hey! Easy! Calm down, you two!" A guy—I'd say he's nineteen, maybe twenty—paces into the dim light of the alleyway. His voice is soft, almost calming, quite the opposite of his tall, muscular stature.

This changes things.

The young, dark-skinned man wears a serious expression as he steps toward the guards, hands held pacifyingly in the air. His eyes meet mine for a beat, but he turns his head to the guards, running his fingers through his carefully trimmed, curly brown hair.

"Come on," he says. "Lower your weapons. Look at the clothes they just threw down. They're obviously homeless defectors."

Defectors? What's that?

I glance at Lacy and give her a tilt of my head to follow my lead. As the young man continues to argue on our behalf, I slowly start toward them, moving inch by inch, hardly noticeable at all.

"Being homeless isn't an excuse for breaking the law!" the male guard yells.

The guy, for some reason, continues to argue our case. "I'll get them to return the clothes and I'll pay for the window myself. There's no need to—"

"Oh, shut up," the woman snaps, scrambling for a comm. "I'm contacting the EHC station right now!"

"You could stand to have a little pity for people like this," the guy argues, keeping their attention from us as Lacy and I creep closer to the guards. I nod to her, and in one swift motion we bolt in their direction. The guys follow our lead. I grab the man, and Lacy lunges for the woman. I snatch his weapon and throw the guard to the ground. Sky and Drape mow our innocent attempted-rescuer down.

I swing around, weapon in hand, and find Lacy with the female guard in a headlock.

I train my gun at the male guard's head. He freezes. "Get in the car." I wave the weapon at the vehicle. "Now."

We rip off their comms and toss them down. The devices smack against the hard surface and I finish the job by crushing them with my boot. Drape reaches through the busted window, fiddling around, eventually unlocking the vehicle's doors. We shove the two guards into the third row. Lacy squeezes in the back, the pistol pointed at the woman's side.

"You're flying," I tell the guy who tried to help us, directing him into the driver's seat. A part of me wishes I knew how to operate the vehicle, but I don't feel like killing us all today just because I want to test out my new cognitive ability. I scramble into the passenger's seat, continuing to threaten him with the weapon. Sky and Drape climb in behind us with the old clothes and the bag of food. At least the two of them are good for something.

"Let's get this thing in the air. What's your name?" I ask the young man.

He frowns at me, but doesn't seem nearly as bothered by the situation as the two guards. You would think that becoming a hostage right after offering your assistance would make you much more upset, but he seems calm.

"Elias," he says.

"Elias, I'm going to need you to get us moving."

He sighs and awakens the machine.

"Whoa…" Drape gasps nervously as the vehicle lifts from the ground. Nausea spins in my stomach. I gulp to push it down as the lights of the city get smaller out the window.

Pull it together, Fin. You've made it this far. Puking isn't the best confidence builder.

"Wow! This is incredible!" Lacy says from the back row.

Idiot.

"What?" the male guard snarls. "So dirt poor that you've never been inside a craft? Surely you scum have at least taken public transportation?"

"Don't talk to him, Lacy," I snap, knowing their insults will set her off. The last thing we want is for these people to find out we're dwellers. They can keep believing we're homeless defectors— whatever that is.

"Where are we headed?" Elias asks once we're hovering high above the nearby rooftops.

Sky leans forward and growls, "EHC station. Now."

"I don't understand," Elias says.

I know what Sky has in mind. The most likely place for the EHC to take his sister would be the nearby station the guards tried to radio.

"Do what he says," I say. "*Now.*"

CHAPTER 9

"Alright, but it's a long flight. It'll be a couple of hours," Elias says, a strange calm in his voice.

"Well, step on it!" Sky snaps. "We're losing time."

Elias eyes me and lets out a frustrated sigh. I turn back to Sky, keeping my gun on Elias. "We all want to get to Cia. That's why we're here. But the authorities are already searching for us, I'm sure, and jetting across the sky at breakneck speeds will make us stick out even more."

Sky groans and flops back in his seat.

"Be quiet," Lacy orders the two guards in the back row.

My stomach lurches at the fact that she's back there waving a gun at them. I glance at the weapon I'm pointing at Elias and lower it a little. Amazing how quickly we went from common theft to kidnapping.

"So, Elias," I say, trying to dump part of my guilt, "why did you try to save us?"

One of the guards scoffs.

"You need to be quiet," Lacy growls.

Elias ignores what's happening in the back. "You're defectors, aren't you?"

"What's a defector?" Sky asks. I shoot him a dirty look. It's like my friends don't get the importance of not revealing who we are.

"What, do you live under a rock?" the male guard taunts.

You have no idea.

"Defectors are citizens who have opposed the way the government treats dwellers," Elias says, staying cool. I have no idea how he's doing it. "Because of their political views, most defectors wind up homeless or cast out of their families or chased away by local government officials. It never felt right to me."

"What do you mean?" I ask.

"Well…" He pauses. "I guess since my parents were Noble class, I haven't had to deal with poverty. I feel like I have the means to help, so sometimes I do."

"Noble class?" Drape asks.

A quizzical expression overtakes Elias' face. "As in top level citizens."

"There are different levels of citizens?" I ask.

The guards snicker. They must think we're absolute fools, but I don't allow it get to me.

"Yes," Elias says slowly.

"What are the different levels for?"

He shakes his head, still confused. "Nobles buy their way to privilege. Private schools, the nicest neighborhoods, and an upgraded modification—both strength and intelligence."

"So, if you have enough credits, you can be a Noble?" I ask.

"No, not necessarily. You also have to be genetically compatible with the upgraded mod."

"Okay," I say, my ears perking up at the *'genetically compatible'* part. "Then what about everyone else?"

"The standard strength upgrade costs less. If citizens have the money, most of them will use it to become Century class. But Tenant class is normal, able to adapt to the climate and withstand radiation. No upgrades. They're the working class—you know, like, servants. Defectors tend to escape out of the Tenant class."

That's why we were able to one-up the train employees so easily. They were just third-class citizens. No enhanced strength or intelligence. The real question, though, is how *I* managed to get improved intelligence.

"So, if Tenants are the working class, what do Century citizens do?" Lacy asks curiously. She must be realizing that her genetic modification would land her in that class if we weren't dwellers.

"Mostly law enforcement. Police," Elias explains.

I instinctively glance back at the guards. They're probably level two citizens, based on their careers. I can imagine what they would think if they found out a bunch of dwellers had been enhanced right into their citizen classification.

"And Noble class?" I ask.

110

"The designated leader class," Elias says. "The rich snobs."

"Glad you're *aware* of your snobby stature," the female guard scoffs.

Elias shoots her a look over his shoulder before returning his attention to the skies ahead. "So... I've answered your questions. Why don't you tell me where you people are *really* from? You're not from Reso—or anywhere civilized—to have never heard of the classification levels."

"Get us to our destination, then we'll talk," I snap back, remembering we are *not* friends. The promise to talk later is a lie. I have no intention of letting any of these people in on who we are.

He nods, but by his pinched expression, it wasn't the answer he'd hoped for.

Grunts and a scuffling sound come from behind, and I look over my shoulder to see the guards charging Lacy.

Oh crap.

The entire craft tilts to the right, pulling me forward again and crashing my body into the passenger hatch.

"Get off!" Lacy barks.

"All of you need to stay calm!" Elias shouts back.

A *clank* followed by a discharge grabs my full attention. My heart leaps into my throat. I spin in my seat, expecting to see Lacy dead, but it's nearly worse.

The female guard has been shot in the head. Red spatters the side window, a partial divider preventing the mess from covering everything.

The male guard screams and grapples for Lacy's wrist in a desperate attempt to prevent himself from being next. Lacy's like a wild animal freshly uncaged.

"Lacy, stop!"

Not even thinking, I scramble back into the second row, jumping into Sky's lap to get at her. In a flash, I raise my pistol and bash the man in the back of the head. He slumps over, limp.

"You killed her!" I scream at Lacy.

She gasps and stares at the very deceased woman. "I did? I don't even remember doing it… She was just coming at me!"

"What did you do?" Elias yells from the front seat. "She's *dead*?"

I hold out my hand to Lacy. "Give me that gun. *Now!*"

Lacy's eyes go large for a moment as she glances at the bloody mess beside her again. She hands me the gun with a shaking hand. I crawl back over Drape and Sky, who don't say a word, to the front passenger's seat, both guns in tow. My thoughts race.

What just happened?

Elias grips the wheel of the craft so fiercely his knuckles go white. The craft is descending. I point one of the weapons at his side.

"No," I warn him. "Keep flying."

Glancing back, Sky and Drape, their eyes wide, seem mortified, but Lacy is quiet. Almost blank. I catch her eye and shake my head, ashamed.

"I didn't have a choice," Lacy pleads. "They went for the gun. Both of them."

"I saw that gleam in your eye, Lacy! What was *that*?"

"I... I don't know!"

"The modification..." I mumble. "It changed you."

"I...I didn't mean to," she cries and throws her head into her hands.

"Wha... what do you want me to do?" Elias asks, his voice shaking.

"We have to get rid of the guards," Sky says, snapped out of his shock. "Dump the body and drop off the man while he's knocked out."

"Yes," I agree. "In a safe place where we won't get caught... but also where they'll be found soon." I'm not looking for another death on my head. I sit upright in my seat, heaving in shallow breaths. I gag and quickly push back the sensation.

From the side, Elias stares in my direction.

"What?" I snap.

"You didn't want this," he whispers, glancing back at Lacy in horror, then flicking his gaze ahead.

"No," I say. "No, we didn't. Now bring us somewhere safe, Elias."

"I don't have a choice, do I?" He's quiet for a moment. "There's a Tenant class housing sector just outside of Reso. There's not a lot of regular monitoring or operative influence out that way compared to the rest of the city."

"Fine. Take us there." I press the barrel of the gun deeper into his side. "And you better not be lying to us."

In about ten minutes, we make our way just outside of the main stretch. It's completely dark this far out, and with the glow of our craft's front lights, I can barely see the change in the barren landscape that is this housing district. Elias lands several yards from the group of homes. We exit, and I have him walk ahead of us with his hands on his head as we search around.

Lacy rushes to my side. "I feel better now. Hand me back my gun so I can keep an eye on our pilot while you ditch the escort guards."

I glare at her. "Are you kidding? No way."

"You don't *trust* me now?" she asks, hurt brewing in her eyes, as if she's completely forgotten what just happened.

"Can I?" I hiss, turning my back to her.

I take a second to breathe in the landscape. Tall poles with lighting atop them brighten small homes made of stone or brick, nothing like the sleek infrastructures of the city, but they're better than anything I've ever seen underground. There's no vegetation here—mostly red clay and similarly colored sand. I feel as though I've stepped into another world, though I guess I actually have.

"Let's see if we can find a place to dump them," I say, moving further from the hover car. I'm ready to be done with the escort guards as soon as possible. If only I could go back and undo this entire day. Surely there's someone out there who loves and cares about the poor woman. The whole mistake makes me sick.

Click, click.

My heart vaults and I snap my attention to a sizable crowd inching out from around the nearby structures. Their weapons are pointed at my friends and me.

I grit my teeth and glare back at Elias. "Traitor."

But it's not like I can blame him.

CHAPTER 10

"Whoa. Easy, everyone. Easy!" Elias says, raising his hands in the air.

I leave one gun in my hand. The gun I took from Lacy is in my pocket, the handle sticking out an inch. This crowd is impressive. I can't tell exactly how many there are due to the dark, but I suspect close to two dozen.

Elias continues to plead our case. "Calm down! No need for anyone to get hurt!"

A man, maybe in his forties or fifties, steps apart from the crowd. There's a distinct resemblance between him and Elias, no doubt rendering them related.

"Elias!" the man calls out, relief evident in his tone.

Elias smiles briefly, but continues to hold up his hands in an attempt to settle the crowd.

Why is he still *helping us?*

The man swings his attention to me, eying the weapon in my hand and the one in my pocket. "Toss your guns aside, so no one gets hurt."

This needs to end. I throw the gun in my hand onto the dirt away from us and slowly reach for the other one.

"Easy, now," the man says, not taking his attention from me.

I pinch the handle and fling it away like it's burned me.

Several in the crowd slowly lower their weapons as the older man moves in for a hug from Elias. My heart lifts.

Suddenly, Lacy darts the way of the crowd. "Come on!" she roars. "Bring it on!"

What is the matter with her?

I freeze, not willing to follow her with this many guns pointed my way. Visions of my friend being gunned down in this strange land swirl in my head.

Zzzzap sounds from the right, and Lacy falls limply to the ground with a *thump*. I flinch as the noise sounds again, twice, and the boys do the same. I move back and a hot jolt of electricity shudders through me. My vision blurs.

"Zap her again!" a male voice commands as I crumple to my knees. My head spins with pain as I lurch forward into the abyss.

My brain pounds like it's been whacked with a hammer. I try to push myself up, but the world spins and I collapse onto my back again. I blink to clear the swirling ceiling above me, and it slowly winds to a stop.

I turn and scan the space. The lamps are out, but there's a bit of light creeping in from under the door, outlining Sky, Drape, and Lacy lying on the floor near me. Their wrists are bound. My mind clears somewhat and I glance down at myself. My hands are secured, too.

As my vision adjusts, I study the small space. It's filled with crates and plastic bins; a sort of storage room.

I sit upright and moan. My body feels like I fell off a cliff. Ignoring the pain, I kick a leg out in front of me and whack Lacy in her shoulder.

"Get up you piece-of-crap friend," I growl.

She groans and rolls to her side, waking Sky and Drape. The three of them all struggle to sit, just as dazed as I was when I came to.

"What is *wrong* with you?"

"What?" she says.

"Don't you *'what'* me. You darted at a bunch of people with *guns*. You're lucky they didn't kill us all. Seriously, what were you *thinking*?"

"I'm stronger than I've ever been," she says. "I could've pounded them if that one guy didn't surprise me. Elias conned us into coming here and look where it got us."

"Most of these people are probably stronger too!" I shout.

"Elias said this was a Tenant class settlement, you know? So they're not strong like *us*. Well, if he was telling the truth, that is." She takes a quick scan around. "Great. Well, we're in trouble now."

"Thanks to *you*." If my hands weren't tied, they'd be wringing her neck. "None of this would have happened if you had just let us go home after our shift."

"I'm done with being the underdog," she protests, shame peppering her words.

"Guys, shh," Sky hushes us, but I don't care who hears what at this point. Lacy shoots me a death glare.

The door creaks open. My eyes lock on the man who greeted Elias when we landed. He flicks on the lamp and I squint. He's a firm-faced man with tender brown eyes, much like Elias, but his paler complexion seems to shine from the light layer of sweat on his brow. This and his stubbly black and gray beard, along with his small but noticeable extra weight, give him the appearance of a working man.

"You four sure do know how to make an entrance," he says. His beautiful white teeth and cynical grin make me lower my eyes. His expression, though, has that same gentleness I noticed in Elias'.

"Let us go," Lacy says.

I throw a kick her way and bare my teeth to let her know she has lost the privilege to speak or act on our behalf. She relents. Mission accomplished.

"Who are you?" I ask the man.

"Mason." He kneels in front of us, maintaining a safe distance. "I'm a supervisor here at this settlement."

"Told you. Nothing but Tenants or whatever here," Lacy mutters.

I hear a chuckle coming from the doorway. Elias enters carrying a tray with food and water. "You'd think that, wouldn't you?"

Mason shakes his head. "Elias..." he says sternly.

"What? They won't say anything. They're on the run from the EHC. I doubt they'll tattle on us." He turns to me. "My Uncle Mason is a Noble like me. He just doesn't like anyone from here to know."

I flick an *'I told you so'* look at Lacy, but she avoids my gaze.

Elias sets the tray of food on the floor in the middle of us. Lacy doesn't wait even one second to snatch up her share, even with both hands bound on her lap.

"Sorry about lying to you four about why I wanted to come out this way, but you did shoot a woman," Elias continues, his eyes lowered. "You can't blame me for getting nervous."

"No, we can't. It was a smart move," I say before Lacy has a chance to swallow her mouthful of food and make a smart-mouthed comment.

"So, are you EHC defectors from the outer sectors?" Elias asks.

"Yes," I say firmly. Mason and Elias exchange glances as if they're having a silent conversation. Sky, Drape, and even Lacy all seem to have decided to keep their traps shut and allow me to do the talking. Good.

"Well, this makes more sense now," Elias says. "I'm sorry."

"Why would you be sorry? We're the ones who kidnapped you."

"My uncle and I help defectors," Elias explains. "Though, we're usually much quieter about it. It can't be easy what you're going through."

"Okay, that's enough, Elias," Mason insists.

But I'm not satisfied with the little information he's given me. "Why are you here with a group of Tenants if you're a top-level EHC?" I ask Mason.

Mason scowls and doesn't answer.

"My uncle can't stand working with the EHC elite."

"Because they're a bunch of manipulative swine," Mason adds, crossing his arms and leaning his back against the far wall. He inhales deeply and glances at me. "We took care of the dead guard. The other one we have locked up until we can decide what to do with him. You're lucky Elias is an excellent pilot. Anyone else would have crashed with all the ruckus he tells me went on during your flight."

"Why would you dump a body for us?" I ask, shocked. "You don't owe us anything."

"Believe me, I am not thrilled about it," Mason says. "I'm not a fan of violence, and I'm ashamed a life has been taken, but those guards are a threat to our beliefs. We do our best to stay out of the way of the elite, but you gave us no choice."

"What does a supervisor *do*?" I ask Mason curiously.

He doesn't answer, and Elias speaks on his behalf again. "My uncle is in charge of this settlement and its people."

"Yeah, I get that, but what does that *mean*?"

Elias looks at me like I should know, but he answers me nonetheless. "He receives orders from the EHC—assignments for the settlement. His job is to make sure they're followed. Now, I've been honest and answered your questions. It's your turn to answer mine. What are your names?"

I hesitate. I could lie. My heart pounds as I open my mouth. "Fin. This is Drape, Sky, and Lacy."

"Ask the real questions, Elias." Mason locks onto me. "Why in the world would a bunch of defectors try to go to an EHC operative base? Ops are not exactly known to be friendly to your kind."

"They have my sister," Sky says. "Nero Kyoto took her and headed here."

Mason grimaces. "Ugh, *Kyoto*? That guy is on a quest to prove himself. Mercilessly stomping out anyone not in line with the ideologies of the EHC."

"Why?" I ask.

"To prove he's worthy, I guess. He was at the bottom of his class when he enrolled. Worked his way up and took out anyone or anything that stood in his way."

"But why would they bring her to Reso?" Elias asks. "It's not exactly protocol for how they handle combatants, let alone children."

"We were traveling to Reso. We were just outside of the city when they nabbed her," I say quickly. None of us know the names of many cities on the surface. I don't want us to talk ourselves into a corner.

"What did Kyoto want with her?" Mason asks.

"She stole food," I lie. "A trivial crime that he seems rather bent on punishing a child for."

"That sounds like the EHC," Elias snarls. "Heartless."

Mason releases a long sigh, and he and Elias exchange glances, seemingly having another one of their silent conversations. Eventually Mason nods and then turns his attention back to us.

"What is your sister's name?"

"Cia," Sky says. "And she's all I got."

"Settle down. We're looking to help you, but you have to promise that we can trust you. No more firearms." He points at Lacy. "Especially not for this one."

Lacy huffs.

"You can trust us," I insist. "And believe me, after today, I wouldn't allow her near a weapon."

"Good. Then we are in agreement." Mason taps his nephew's shoulder. "Let's untie them and get them to the sleeping quarters. Give them back their belongings they came with, too."

They untie us and we trail Elias and Mason out of the storage room, but not before we each grab the bread they brought us and scarf it down. With her eyes, Lacy questions whether or not we're going to attempt to overpower them. I shake my head firmly. I'm starting to wonder if she's completely lost it.

Elias tosses me the bag of chocolate bars and snacks we took from the transport shuttle. I look inside to see if it's all still there. It is. He grins almost as if he knows how incredibly rare and special it is for us.

We walk across the way toward a large, lengthy building with a rounded roof. No more than the light of a few street lamps brightens the way—who knows what time of night it is.

Inside the building, the quarters are arranged in a barracks-like way with two rows of bunk beds. I jump as a loud snoring comes from one of the beds beside me. A head peeks out from the upper bunk. I scan the space and find there are several people already asleep in here. Mason and Elias lead us to a corner away from the sleepers.

"Why are you doing this?" Sky whispers as Mason pulls a couple of spare blankets out of a storage closet.

"I don't like the way society is run around here. Or anywhere," Mason answers. "The world post-Flip is not a kind one. The societal classes are cruel, especially for the dwellers—the non-mods. It makes me sick."

"And you feel the same way, Elias?" I ask.

"Yes. My dad died when I was young. I was mostly raised by my mom—my Uncle Mason's sister. She was always kind to defectors when no one else would be, but she was never as strong as Mason. She still lives as a member of the elite. I do, too, when I'm with her, but now I'm there just to keep an eye on her. To keep her safe."

Mason pats one of the bunks. "All right. Two of you can sleep on this bunk, and then right across the way, those bunks are free, too. We'll regroup in the morning and see what we can do about locating your sister."

Sky smiles. "Thank you, sir. You have no idea how much that means to me."

Mason gives Sky a subtle grin, then clasps his nephew's shoulder. "Off to sleep."

"Yes, sir." Elias follows his uncle out. When they're gone, I glance at Sky. A worried expression fills his face.

"We need to rest," I urge him. "We'd be no good to your sister now after the day we've had."

He agrees, but doesn't seem all that satisfied. I guess I wouldn't be either.

The boys take the beds across the way. Lacy looks at me as if she has something to say and doesn't want to.

"What?" I ask.

She pinches her lips together, then leans toward my ear. "I didn't mean to kill that woman. It's just… I thought she was going to get the gun. It all happened so fast."

I sigh and pull back from her. "I don't know what to say. It's not like I can tell you it was okay. You need to be more careful. *All* our lives are at stake here. Other people's lives, too."

She hangs her head for a second, then looks up at the bunk. "I get the top."

"Great avoidance strategy, Lacy." I wave my hand, indicating the upper bed. "Be my guest."

She scurries up and buries herself under the blankets. I fall into the bottom bunk, still clutching my precious bag of food and trying to push away the nightmare of today. My body wants to naturally curl up into this lovely bed, far more comfortable than anything I've ever slept on in the sleeping quarters below ground.

Lacy pops her head over the edge. "You still got that candy?"

"We should ration it," I reply, holding the sack tighter.

"No way. That Mason guy will probably give us some more food."

I shake my head. I hate to admit it, but I'm sure she's right. "Fine."

I reach into the bag and grab one of the bars and break it in half. Before I even have the chance to hand it to her she's already ripped it from my hand and has it in her mouth. I'm not even sure what happened to the paper.

"I so want to go snoop around this place," she mumbles, mouth full of chocolate.

"Just finish your candy and go to bed." If anyone's ever needed a mother, it's that girl.

She flops over out of sight. There's crackling sounds from above and a moment later the wrapper drops onto the floor. I guess she *didn't* eat it with the chocolate.

I glance over to Sky and Drape across the walkway only to realize they're staring back at me.

"Can we have some, too?" Drape pleads.

I look at the halved chocolate bar in my hands and roll onto my side, flinging it to him. I know if I eat it, it's going to give me a stomach ache. "You can split that."

Apparently because Drape doesn't give a care about stomach aches, he breaks it in half and hands one of the pieces to Sky.

"Fin? I said I wasn't sharing with them," Lacy gripes from above.

"That was my half. You have no say."

Sky's lips quirk into a weak smile as he looks my way. Quickly, he leans back and peels open the wrapper.

Drape's eyes are closed, chocolate already smeared across his face. I open my mouth to let him know but he rolls over, away from me. Cleaning his face is the least of his worries, I guess.

Sky's just staring up at the underside of the top bunk, nibbling on the corner of his treat.

"Hey," I whisper to him. "You okay?"

He blinks from his trance and twists to face me. "Oh, sorry. I… I just can't stop thinking about her. She's probably so scared. She's never been alone for this long. I've always been there to tuck her into bed. It's just… *hard*, ya know?"

My mind works through today's events. It feels like getting off our shift happened a lifetime ago. Why did I have to listen to Lacy today? Nine times out of ten, I tell her no. This had to be the one time I said yes to her. How did *any* of this happen?

I push back the negative thoughts and straighten with false confidence. "We're going to get her back. We didn't come this far for nothing. Elias and Mason will help us."

"I don't know. This world we're in is so new. We don't know what to expect or who to trust. I'm all Cia has."

"She has us now, too," I say, forcing myself to believe it.

The bunk above me rattles. "Quit yappin', I'm tired," Lacy whines.

I kick the underside of her bed. "You're such a punk, Lacy."

"Yeah, but you love me anyway."

I turn back to Sky, but he's turned over, facing the other way now. I guess he's done talking. I don't blame him. He's a good guy and he has a good heart.

I adjust my soft pillow and tuck my forearm under it. Facing the wall gives me a bit of privacy from the room filled with strangers and my friends. It doesn't take long before the room fades.

∞

Screeeech.

I jolt. My head thwacks on the wooden underside of the bunk above me as I sit up. I curse under my breath and throw my feet to the floor.

"What is that?" I snap. Drape, Sky, and Lacy are already out of bed. Other people are scattering and darting out of the building. Mason rushes into the room and heads straight for us.

"Come with me. Hurry!"

In a flash, he hustles us out the door. I don't even have time to grab my bag of rations. A crack of sunlight peeks over a mountain range in the distance. An enormous, shadowy hovercraft, backlit by the sun, zips our way.

"What's going on?" I demand.

"It's a random EHC security check." Mason's eyes are wide with panic. "We normally have one about every month, but we just had one last week! We're not ready." He looks around, frantic. "Over here now. Hurry!"

He leads us to a few wooden barrels outside of the storage shack we had been in the night before. He opens up the two barrels. "Can two of you fit in one?"

"We'll make it work," I say.

He waves a finger in my face. "Don't show your face until they're gone. Otherwise, we're all dead."

Lacy and I squeeze into one barrel, and the guys into the other. Good thing Drape's built like a twig.

Mason closes the lids. "If you're praying folks, you should get on your knees," he whispers.

Not really sure I could do that even if I wanted to in here.

There's a hole in our barrel, and I peer out of it as the hovercraft lands in the middle of the settlement.

"This is tight," Lacy gripes as her knee makes contact with my chin.

I reach out and grip her by her shirt. "You need to be quiet," I order.

She goes silent, but I can feel the fear radiating from her body.

Outside, Mason stands with a crowd of his people, waiting for the operatives to exit the ship.

"Why do you think they're doing another security check on them?" Lacy whispers.

"Seriously? They're searching for the missing tech," I say.

"And us," she adds.

"And us." I continue peering out the hole. The operatives swarm the entire compound, and I can hear screams.

"I see you've been housing more defectors," one of the operatives yells at Mason as a group of ten men and women are dragged off. "We can't stand by while these people corrupt our society."

"They're just *people*," Mason protests.

"People are powerful if you let them get away with thinking," the operative responds. "Turn this place upside down!"

Operatives continue to swarm and several other defectors are dragged onto the ship. An op runs up to the man who spoke to Mason, whispering in the leader's ear. The man that seems to be in charge one-eighties, throwing out his arm. His fist makes contact with Mason's jaw with a *crack*, knocking him down. I suck in air as several operatives surround him and begin violently kicking Elias' uncle.

Lacy throws me a stunned expression. Though she can't see what's happening, by the noise, I'm certain she can figure it out.

"Please, stop! You're hurting him!" Elias' voice sounds from nearby, but I can't see him from the position of the barrel.

"What's happening?" Lacy whispers.

The male guard we kidnapped, escorted by the operatives, comes into view. "There were four of them—defectors," the guard snarls. "Two girls and two boys. One of them killed my partner!"

The lead op waves his thumb behind him to the crowd of defectors led to the ship. "Any of them?" he asks.

"No," the guard replied.

The lead operative glares down at Mason. "Where are they?"

"I don't know," Mason says as he gasps for breath. He gets kicked in the head for his response. The shocked crowd of people wait frozen around him. None of them want to be next. "I said I don't know, you idiots!" he shouts.

The men lunge for him again, kicking and punching. When they're done, the men violently yank him up to his feet, covered in blood, and drag him to the ship. My heart sinks as I watch.

The lead operative waves his hand at the crowd. "Take this as a lesson. The EHC does *not* put up with traitors! Your leader is coming on a little ride with us."

He turns and marches onto the hovercraft, dragging Mason. Within seconds, the ship lifts from the ground and disappears into the distance, taking Mason with it.

CHAPTER 11

Lacy squirms, trying to see out of the hole in the barrel. "What just happened?"

I shove her back with my shoulder. "They took Mason." My voice shakes. "They beat him to a pulp, then they took him."

"We have to get out of here, Fin," she whispers. "Let's get Drape and leave this place."

"What are you talking about?" Pressure builds in my chest. I know exactly what she's getting at.

"We don't *know* Sky. Why are we doing this for him? And this Elias guy? We basically got his uncle killed. No way he's *not* going to turn us in now."

Everything that's happened over the last day runs through my brain, and again I'm overwhelmed with regret. "Don't be a jerk, Lacy. For once in your life, try to think about anyone but yourself."

"I *am* thinking of other people," she hisses. "*My* people, you and Drape. *You* are the ones I care about and I'm tired of being kicked around. I finally have the upper hand on something and you want to take it away."

I twist my body till our noses nearly touch. "We started something, and we need to finish it. I won't have Cia's life hanging over my head, and I'm certainly not leaving Sky out here. If you want to go, then go, but you're on your own. Drape is coming with me."

Lacy parts her mouth, then snaps it shut. She nods, but avoids my eyes, which is kind of impressive considering there's really nowhere else to look inside this barrel.

I peek out of the hole. The ship is long gone and most of the people at the camp have scattered. There are three or four individuals drifting in and out of sight. I push off the lid of the barrel and drag myself out, my knee whacking into what must be Lacy's head. I don't even say sorry.

As we emerge, the attention of those in the yard snap to us. One short guy with dark hair opens his mouth like he's about to say something, but I cut him off.

"Where's Elias?"

The guy points to one of the outer buildings.

Out of the corner of my eye, Drape and Sky emerge from their hiding spot. I swing toward them and wave to the building the man pointed out. I look at Lacy. "You're with us, right?"

She pinches her lips together. "I'm not leaving you, Fin."

The tension in my chest releases. For as awful as Lacy has been, she's still my best friend, and I love her like a sister. I guess, anyway. If I knew what having a sister was *like*.

I smack my hand to her upper arm and pull her along with me. Drape and Sky are already out of their hiding places and the four of us race for the meager outbuilding, zig-zagging around the people running around doing who knows what. We burst through the door and Elias is sitting, head in hands, at a small table in the middle of the room.

The space is cramped, with a desk in one corner complete with a computer system. With all our commotion, Elias doesn't even acknowledge us.

I shuffle to the table, and the rest follow. Without a word, I grab for the back of a chair across from Elias and pull it out. The metal legs screech across the floor. The noise makes Elias' head pop up.

"Mason saved us," I say, sitting. "I don't understand why, but he did."

"He did it because he's a good guy. Hard to believe after what you all did last night, but Mason's seen worse out here."

Scenes of the bloody back window roll through my head. I study Lacy, but she's avoiding me.

"He's always known that social change is ugly," Elias continues. "But I don't think I understood it until this morning." He releases a long sigh and turns his attention to Sky. "I'll make you a deal. I want to help you find your sister. I'll take you all to the EHC operative base and help locate the girl."

Sky drops into the seat beside me.

"But," Elias adds, "you have to help me find my uncle there. If he's alive, that's the location they've got him. It's the only way I'll do it."

Sky's jaw is tense and Drape's pacing behind me, white as a ghost, probably in shock. Lacy's leaned up against the doorway, arms crossed over her chest.

"We can do that," I agree, "but know our mission is Cia first. Mason saved us. He could have given us up, but he didn't. However, Sky's sister is the reason we're doing this. I need you to know that now because if it comes down to it, we won't risk Cia's safety for your uncle."

"Fine," he says. "I can deal with your terms, but I need your word about my uncle."

I don't wait for the others before saying, "You have it."

Sky reaches out his hand and Elias takes it. "So how do we get there?" Sky asks.

Elias shakes and releases Sky's hand. "We'll use the hovercar you all stole, land just outside their airfield, and go the rest of the way on foot."

"Sounds like a plan to me," I say. "Let's go get Cia and Mason."

We exit the office and head back to the storage shack. Elias walks indoors, signaling us to wait where we are.

"You ready for this?" I ask Sky.

"I have to be," he says, straightening his shoulders. "Elias is our best bet at finding Cia."

"You trust him?" I press since I'm not sure Sky is the kind of guy who trusts anyone but himself.

"He hasn't provided us a single reason not to." He furrows his brow in thought. "We've given him plenty."

Before I have the chance to answer, Elias exits with a large black duffle bag thrown over his shoulder.

"What's in there?" Lacy asks.

Elias avoids eye contact with her and keeps his attention on me. "Weapons, and if it works for you, I'd like to leave them in the duffle bag until we get to the base. I don't want a certain person getting her hands on them."

Lacy scoffs, but I ignore her. He's right.

"Your weapons. Your call," I say.

He guides us to a small cave just on the outskirts of the settlement. The hovercar is hidden inside and he pops open the pilot's door. "I trust it will be a more pleasant experience this round?" He glares at Lacy.

"Yes," she sighs. "But I'm not sitting in the back." She hops into the second row. "It's cleaner up here."

The words send a painful jolt from my gut to my chest. Her indifference to the guard's death is not the Lacy I know. She sprawls out and lies down, taking up the entirety of the row. She rests her head on the far side door, her hands underneath her neck, and shuts her lids. Apparently she intends on taking a nap.

Drape pleads at me with his eyes. There's no way he wants to sit in the back. Blood makes him queasy.

"Drape, sit up front with Elias," I order to prevent him having to have an embarrassing conversation about his weak stomach.

He flashes me a thankful grin and climbs into the passenger seat. Sky and I climb into the back row together. I cringe as I sit close to the bloodied window. A member of the settlement must've attempted to scrub the mess away, but it's still caked in every crevice that lines the paneling near the window. The smell of the cleaner churns my stomach, reminding me of the rare times we'd be allowed fruit for our meals underground, always more than a few days past ripe.

The hovercar lifts into the air and darts from the cave entrance.

"Okay," Elias says once we're headed away from the camp. "Settle in. It's a bit of a flight to the base since it's on the opposite end of the city."

"Seriously?" Lacy whines.

Elias glances back at her. "Um, yeah?"

"Ignore her. She's just in a foul mood because you won't let her near the duffle bag." I shoot her a dirty look, but she already has her eyes shut again. "She can be trying when she hasn't had her beauty sleep."

"So that's what was wrong with her yesterday," Elias says bitterly.

I don't answer.

With Lacy sleeping, the rest of us grow quiet. Drape and Elias whisper up front, wrapped up in conversation I strain to hear, but can't. I can only hope Drape is smart enough not to allow anything to slip that adds to Elias' suspicions.

Sky slouches in his seat and gazes out his blood-free side window

"Cia will be fine," I say, keeping my voice down.

"You don't know that," he whispers, frowning.

"Well, we're going to do whatever we can to make this right. It's special what you and your sister have. I've never had that. The closest thing I have to that is Lacy and Drape."

"You really don't have any family?"

"None that I know of," I say, glancing up to the front of the aircraft to assure myself Elias is distracted by his conversation with Drape. "I grew up in the Oven, remember?"

Sky looks at me as though I'm the one to be sympathized with. A part of me wonders if that's true.

"What was it like growing up in the mines?" he asks softly.

"Mentally draining and hard on the body. A lot of work for nothing. Work for your rations. Work or die, basically. It's all I ever knew. If you wanted more than the minimum, you had to take it. That's what we did. We stole from the shipping facility to try to better our lives just a little, and now it's gotten us into this mess."

"I'm sorry," Sky says. "I mean, making sure we had enough to supplement our garden was hard at times—especially when our garden didn't produce enough—but I was free, you know? You... you weren't."

"No, I wasn't. But the sad part is, I didn't realize it until I met you." I slouch down similarly to how he is, propping my shins against the seat ahead of me. His life sounds like something out of a dream. No orders from mining bosses, and unlike me he knows where he came from.

A slight smile appears on his lips. "It took me awhile, but I get you. I really do. I'm glad you're here... here with me."

I feel his hand gently brush up alongside mine. He blushes and yanks it away quickly as he clears his throat.

I smile back at him, trying to hide the flush creeping up my neck. "Yeah, I guess so."

"We're nearly there," Elias says.

Beep. Beep.

The sound comes from the pilot display panel. My heart jolts. Sky and I lean forward onto the next seat.

"What's that?" I ask.

Lacy sits up, draping her arms over the front seat.

"We're getting an alert," Elias says.

As if on cue, two wide flying machines zip up toward us, one on either side.

"What are those?" Drape asks.

"Um… haven't you seen EHC security drones?" Elias asks, hitting the controls on the panel.

The beeping on the display stops and a female voice comes through. "Attention. Please come to an immediate halt."

Elias breathes deeply and slows down the hover car. The two drones track us and hover on either side of the vehicle.

Elias speaks into the control panel. "Is there a problem?"

"Why are you flying so near the operative base?" the voice questions. "Please state your business immediately."

"Um…" Elias mumbles, but then speaks clearly and firmly. "Our hover car is damaged, and this outpost was the closest safe landing zone. We could use assistance."

There's a long pause on the other line. Hopefully, the person is speaking with someone in charge about Elias' request.

The voice returns. "Please follow the drones. They will escort you to a holding bay where your vehicle can be properly assessed."

"Will do, and thank you," Elias says politely.

"Cut the commlink," I whisper.

Elias presses a button on the display to prevent the people manning the drones from hearing us. Glaring into the rearview, Elias' eyes lock on Lacy with intensity. "I've *never* been stopped this far out from the base," he snarls. "A handful of troublesome defectors would never ramp up the EHC this much. Between this and the second surprise inspection this month, what did you four do?"

Lacy throws me a warning glance, her nostrils flared. We need his help, but we're also risking his life. Elias has no idea what he's gotten himself into, but we're in too deep.

"We don't have time for this now," I say. "You and I know we can't keep tailing these drones. As soon as we land, they'll find us out."

"Fine," Elias growls. "It barely matters anymore. I may not be a defector, but when they realize I'm Mason's nephew, they'll question why I'd be snooping around here right after his arrest. I'm probably dead anyway."

"So what's the plan?" Drape asks.

"Something stupid." Elias grips the steering mechanism tight. "Brace yourselves." He flips the communication beacon back on. "Mayday, Mayday!" he shouts into the display and cuts the power.

My jaw drops, but not as quickly as the craft. Screams fill the cab. Sky grabs my hand, and I squeeze back. The car spins into a nosedive to the earth.

"We should have never trusted this guy!" Lacy screams.

The makeshift cover Mason's people fastened over the hole isn't the best, and a whirlwind of paper and scattered belongings whip past my head and out the busted back window.

The events of the last twelve hours careen through my head. We braved a backbreaking climb, jumped a train, stole a vehicle, and killed a woman all to save a kid we don't know, and this is how it ends.

CHAPTER 12

"Crap!" Drape screams in the same high-pitched tone he had before his voice changed.

The vehicle jolts as Elias cuts the power back on. He yanks on the steering system and we pop up, barely avoiding a collision with the earth below. One of the pursuing drones smashes into a tree and metal flies through the air, nearly slamming into the hover, but then we flip. My screams drown out my friends' as the world spins.

Amazingly, Elias gets us upright.

"I...I..." he stammers, breathless. "I think we shook that drone. Is everyone safe?"

I grip the bloodied seat with one hand and squeeze Sky's hand so tight with the other I feel his knuckles pop. The poor guy has one leg propped up against the door perpendicular to himself, his free hand gripping the seatbelt. Lacy, who must have fastened her seatbelt before Elias nearly killed us all, is flopped over in the second row, whining and swearing at Elias. And then there's poor Drape, gagging. I pray he doesn't lose the contents of his stomach.

Sky and I make eye contact for a moment, and we both yank our hands from one another and sit upright.

Lacy stiffens. "What's wrong with you!" she screams at Elias.

Elias exhales. "We made it."

I bury my head in my hands, curling forward and hoping the action will make the nightmare go away. When I lift up again, the nightmare is still a reality. "Good job," I whisper, but I doubt he even hears me.

Somewhere in the middle of nowhere, the vehicle finally kisses the dirt. I'm about ready to kiss it, too, if I can ever get out.

"Why'd we land?" Lacy asks as we pile out of the craft. "We're not at the base."

Elias swings toward her. "Because searchers will be out scouting for the crashed drone and for us. We can't just waltz in there and hope no one's going to notice."

Lacy backs off as Sky races past her to Elias.

"That was amazing!" Sky says, as if he's totally forgotten that we were all nearly splattered on the ground.

"I mean, did you see how close we were to being munched?" Drape exclaims, checking his body for new injuries.

Sky, a very slight smile on his face, adds, "I swear, Elias, I thought for a minute there we were all dead! That we had just handed the reins to a suicidal nutjob!"

Apparently, he does remember he almost died, but the action has consumed his brain. Boys.

We pass a water canteen from person to person. Only a gulp or two each and it's empty. The heat is unbearable here, but the lukewarm water helps a little. We gather a few supplies, as well as the weapons, and decide to move out. Lacy and I walk at the back of the group, the three guys walking shortly ahead of us.

"Seriously, it just came to me." Elias puffs up his chest. "A part of me has always wanted to try something like that, but wow!"

"Idiots," Lacy growls under her breath, and I laugh. Frankly, I'm enjoying the light-hearted moment. Fun is a foreign concept to dwellers. Fun is stealing and getting away with it. It's certainly not something I expected to have on our rescue mission.

"It's nice to see Sky— I mean... everyone happier," I say, looking at Sky. Where did that come from? I scratch my temple as I glance at him again, strutting ahead of me. Hopefully Lacy didn't notice.

"Whatever." Lacy picks up the pace, catching up to the guys just as Elias and Sky are starting in on Drape for nearly losing his lunch.

"Alright fellas, you've had your fun. Time to get serious," Lacy says. "Elias, we're getting close to the operative base. If they're as guarded as you say they are, there's a chance we'll have to use those weapons of yours. Best to take them out of the bag and show us how to use them."

Elias stops in his tracks and spins, glaring at Lacy. "Yes, I suppose you're right." He puts the bag down, unzipping it and producing a strange-looking weapon with a very long barrel. "You want this one, Lacy?"

"Heck yeah." She reaches for it, but he pulls back and holds his palm up.

"Okay," he says. "It's all yours *if* you can tell me what it's called."

My stomach twists in a knot. It doesn't require a modified genius to figure out what Elias is doing.

"Um, a gun," Lacy says, putting her hands on her hips. She tries to play it off like she's too cool to take his question seriously. "Quit joking around and hand it to me."

"What *kind* of gun?" he asks with a smirk.

"Does it matter? So what if I don't know my guns that well?"

"This is literally one of the most common guns that the operatives use. Everyone knows what this is called," he says, shaking it. "Tell me what it's called, and I'll give it to you."

"I don't know," she growls. "Quit being stupid!"

"Okay, okay, you're right." He hands it to her, a glint in his eye.

Sky, Drape, and I watch as Lacy fumbles with the piece of machinery, obviously having no idea how to even hold it or which end is the front and which is the back. Elias shakes his head and bends down to dig in the bag, pulling out an identical weapon.

A flush travels up my neck, my mind racing at his questions. The only logical reason would be that Elias wants to make sure we tell him who we really are. The clarity in my thoughts rationalizes everything. My mind was on autopilot, as if it was figuring it all out for me.

"It's called a *blaster*. It's what we got you guys with last night," he says and presses his hands around the chamber. The sides light up blue and he twists the barrel and slides his hand forward in a quick motion to fire. A blue, electrical bolt jolts out of it and hits a nearby rock.

Lacy attempts to mimic what he did and fumbles. *Come on blue bolt.* The blaster clicks, but no blue bolt.

Elias snatches it out of her hand and stuffs it into the duffle bag. Lacy pinches her lips together. He slings his bag back over his shoulder and glares at us. "Start talking. You steal clothes from the back of a car; you say you're defectors, but you've never even heard of the class system; you've never been in a hovercar; you had no idea what the security drones were; and you don't even know what a blaster is! I'm not an idiot! No way are the EHC operatives freaking out this much about a handful of defectors. You're dwellers."

I almost feel like palming my forehead as Lacy, Sky, and Drape immediately turn to me. They could not possibly be more obvious. I resist the urge and keep my eyes trained on Elias.

"Yes," I mumble.

"*How*?" he asks. "How are you up here and not frying under the radiation?"

"Because of our mod kit," Lacy spits out.

I shake my head. She doesn't know when to shut up. I remove the device from my pocket.

"Whoa," Elias says, stepping my way. "Where… where did you get one of those?"

"What, you've never seen one?" Lacy asks, surprised.

"What? Of course not. Not in real life."

"Then how did *you* get modified?"

"They modify us in utero," Elias explains. "Once the mother knows she's pregnant. The earlier, the greater the likelihood she won't miscarry. But how did you four get your hands on one? I mean, dwellers shouldn't have access to tech like that."

"Screw you!" Lacy shouts. "We have a right to this just as much as you people do! To be able to live on the surface! To see the sun! You have no right to—"

"I didn't mean that you *shouldn't* be allowed," Elias says sharply, cutting her off. "But the elite don't believe you should, and they're careful to hide modification away from dwellers. How'd *you* get it?"

"Well—" Lacy starts, but Drape elbows her and shakes his head to let her know she needs to stop talking. She does.

So I tell Elias everything. I suppose he's gotten us this far, and it's not right to keep him out of the loop. I explain how we came across the mod kit, how Sky's sister was actually kidnapped, and how we managed to climb out of our world and into his. When I'm finished, I wait silently for his response.

He glares at us. "I can't trust any of you. You put my family in danger." Elias releases a lengthy sigh. "But you're right, Lacy. You deserve to see the sun."

He bends down and starts digging through the duffle bag. He tosses each of us a weapon.

"I thought you said you couldn't trust us," Drape says, gripping his blaster.

"I can't," Elias mutters. "But what choice do I have? I need you four just as much as you need me if I want to see my uncle alive again." He stands and offers the weapon for us to see. "Hands here. Press this switch to ready the weapon. Hold here to charge and release to blast."

We copy his movements, sending four bluish blasts into the sides of a small hill.

"Good. It will stun the operatives if we have to use it, but as we get closer to the base, they'll be using guns with bullets like the ones the guards had. They'll shoot to kill."

After our mini lesson, we follow Elias, each armed with a blaster at our side. I'm not sure it makes me feel that much better since we're all silent, brooding in our newfound distrust of one another.

In the distance, the outpost materializes; one giant facility with multiple structures connected together, jutting from a large hillside like a clump of quartz—jagged, but formed together for a single purpose. Dull in color, the structure lacks any ounce of personal flare. Each building that juts out is just a slightly different shade of beige.

We tread softly and quietly toward it. The terrain near us is sparse and we're incredibly exposed, but what else can we do? My mind works to come up with a better plan. *Anything.*

A shuffling sounds from the horizon, and before I can narrow in on it, a bullet screams past us. Adrenaline thrusts me to run.

"Shoot them!" a familiar voice rages, and my eyes lock onto Nero, leading nearly two dozen operatives down a hill fifty or so yards out.

I one-eighty and twist the mechanism on my blaster. The pulse slams into one of the ops and he goes down. "Get back!" I order my friends.

Elias shoots and another op hits the dirt.

"Move!" I bark. "Move, now!"

We don't stand a chance out here in the open. I scan the terrain and spot an enormous rock outcropping. The large rocks are toppled onto one another and there's an opening on the right side. I calculate how quickly we could get there versus how quickly the operatives are pushing in on us. It's worth the risk.

"There!" I yell. "Go!"

It's a considerable sprint, but it isn't as though we have much choice. We bolt, a slew of bullets continuing to zip by. I run faster than I ever have in my life, lungs burning, and I pray that we're not so out of breath by the time we get there that we can't fight back.

As we run, Elias and Lacy provide us with limited cover fire, but now that the operatives know we're mainly sporting blasters, they become more confident and pound at us more quickly. Elias has pistols in his bag, and I wish we'd armed ourselves with those instead. He bolts into the opening in the outcropping first and ducks for cover. I sprint in after him and spin around, sliding on my knees into a position facing our threat. Dust kicks up in the small, dimly lit space.

My stomach drops. Lacy and Sky scurry in after us, dragging Drape. His arms are thrown over each of their shoulders.

"What happened?" I demand as bullets glance off the rocks, chipping away at their surfaces, thudding into the dirt around our makeshift holdup.

"He took a bullet for you, that's what!" Lacy yells.

My heart aches. Blood drips from Drape's shoulder. He doesn't speak as Lacy and Sky sit him down against a boulder, his head bobbing back and forth. Drape's blood drips down the rock and pools in the dirt at the base.

I drop my blaster on the ground in front of me. "He's going to bleed out," I say. "We can't keep this up."

Fear washes through everyone's faces.

"Don't," Drape mutters. "Not for me."

"If we don't, he'll die," I say, swinging my attention to the group.

"We'll *all* die if we surrender," Elias argues, throwing down his black satchel and tossing his weapon away from us. The others toss their guns aside, too.

"Maybe not." I dive for the bag and stash the mod kit inside. In a flash, I claw back a large wedged rock and shove the bag with the extra pistols and the mod kit into a crevasse. I cover it with some smaller stones and nod at my friends. All but Drape throw up their hands in surrender.

Nero's men rush the opening and swarm, guns trained on us. "Secure them," Nero orders. "Time for a little chat at the base."

Well, no one's dead yet, and we *are* headed to our destination. That in itself is a miracle.

CHAPTER 13

"Where is she?" Sky hisses, sweat dripping from his brow.

Nero doesn't say a word. The guards continue marching us forward. Sky grits his teeth and fire blazes in his eyes. He obviously doesn't care for going quietly.

"Where's Cia?" he shouts.

Nero abruptly stops, and with him, the rest of his entourage.

"What did you do to her? I want my sister. Tell me!"

Nero turns slowly on his heels. He cocks his head and smirks as he makes his way over to Sky, taking his sweet time. Finally, he stands face to face with him.

My body feels like it might explode. If I thought I could take this guy out, I would. Sky opens his mouth to speak, but nothing comes out. Evidently there's something about being on the receiving end of Nero's glare that can stun anyone.

"What?" Nero hisses.

"My… my sister," Sky stutters. "What did you do to her?"

Without warning, Nero delivers a fierce punch to Sky's jaw. I suck in a sharp breath. Immediately, two operatives are on Sky, each grabbing one of his arms to hold him in place. Nero delivers several more punches to Sky's face and gut.

"That's enough!" Elias roars. "Leave him alone!"

Surprisingly, Nero listens and drops his arms to his side. A droplet of Sky's blood trickles down one of his wrists. Elias' eyes grow wide as he watches Nero pull out a handkerchief from his back pocket and wipe away the blood.

Nero rounds on Elias, tossing the stained handkerchief down. "You seem familiar." He reaches for a device hanging from his utility belt, then grips Elias' shirt collar, yanking him forward. Nero raises the device up to Elias' eyes and a white beam emits from it. A retinal scan.

"Noble class?" Nero laughs. "What's a Noble citizen doing hanging out with a bunch of filthy slags?"

"Better than a bunch of corrupt leeches like you," Elias spits out.

I cringe, my chest tensing, expecting Nero to go for Elias next. Instead, Nero laughs, then clasps Elias' shoulder. Elias flinches.

"Funny, coming from a fellow leech, right?" Nero says. "Personally, I like the title those dirty little dwellers gave us. I wear it proudly. If you want to belittle yourself by hanging around people like them, so be it."

Nero straightens his shirt and steps past Elias, but Elias isn't finished yet. "The EHC are the ones who are disgusting. Dwellers are people, too. You're nothing more than a heartless tool for the EHC."

Nero shakes his head. "Our concern is for law-abiding citizens, not the unenhanced."

"Law abiding citizens who can *afford* Noble and Century modifications, right?" Elias presses. "You're Noble class, right? As arrogant as you are, you're not just a Century thug."

Nero turns, a wry grin on his lips. "Smart boy. You figured me out."

Why Nero is allowing this to continue, I have no idea. But he's no dummy, and I'm sure it's not because he loves to chat.

"How did a Noble like you wind up being nothing but an operative?" Elias sneers.

I wince, anticipating the attack that has to be looming.

Nero grits his teeth. "I am a head op of the entire Reso sector! Don't underestimate that, you dweller sympathizer!"

"Calling me a sympathizer is not an insult," Elias shoots back.

"Well, good." Nero composes himself and straightens. "Because after this, you'll be lucky to be living among the defectors in the streets. Dwellers—they're only a step above moles. Bunch of pathetic thieves. One day, if we're lucky, the world won't even need their kind anymore."

I catch a glimpse of Sky's bloodied face as it hangs to the side, sending my heart into my stomach.

"Kyoto!" I shout, interrupting his ridiculous back and forth with Elias. "Just tell us if the girl is safe or not."

Nero glances back at me for a moment, but he doesn't bother with eye contact. "She's alive and safe from the radiation, for now."

Sky's voice cracks when he speaks. "Why'd you take her?"

"She's a means to an end. And you four are the end," Nero replies.

"Trust me, this is not over," I insist.

"We'll see about that. Now that we have all of you, I don't see much of a point in keeping the child alive." He pauses. "Unless, of course, you tell me what you did with that mod kit."

At the outside of the base, a guard enters a passcode at two enormous metal doors. The entry cranks open into a huge room full of bustling operatives. Wordlessly, they lead us down several hallways until Nero pauses in front of a door. An operative close to us nearly trips over himself rushing to open it. Evidently Nero is too important to open his own doors.

We enter a space lined with prison cells on either side, all empty.

"I promise you all," Nero says, "we have ways of making our prisoners talk. We always get what we want."

They shove each of us into separate holding cells, except for Drape. He collapses on the floor in the middle of the room, unable to walk a step further.

"Get this piece of trash out of here," Nero orders. The men snap to attention and drag Drape away.

I grip the bars of my cell. "If you hurt him—"

"You'll do what?" Nero's gaze bores into mine, and then he taps the bars. "These are built to withstand all classifications of citizens. You're not getting out of here."

He turns and he and his party of goons exit with Drape.

"Drape!" Lacy calls, whirling to me. "You just *let* them take him?"

"What was I supposed to *do*?"

"They might be bringing him to the medical bay," Elias says.

"Yeah, I'm *sure* that's what they're doing. Come on! We should have *done* something!" Lacy yells.

"We have to stay calm or they'll kill Cia and Drape. Probably kill all of us!" I shout right back.

"If they're torturing her…" Sky's voice shakes. "We need to do something!"

"Calm down," Elias says from the cell across from Sky. "She's just their bartering chip. There's no reason to hurt her. But if Drape tells them what they want to know, they'll kill all of us. Cia included."

Sky drops to his knees, gripping the cell bars. "They can't hurt her. She's all I have."

Elias nods. "I know."

"Sky," I whisper.

He eyes me as I reach my hand through the bars that separate our cells. I try to take his hand, but he pulls away. I look back to Lacy and Elias. Elias is calm and staring at us. Lacy's pacing her cell like a trapped animal.

I jump as the exit doors slam open. Two burly operatives enter and march right up to Elias' cell. Elias moves back, stiffening as the cell door unlocks, his face tense with rage. Without warning, a long stick is driven into his side. An electrical jolt stiffens Elias' body, dropping him to the ground. To my horror, the stockier of the two men needlessly gives him a fierce kick in the gut.

"Leave him alone!" I yell as they drag Elias out of his cell.

The larger of the men grins at me. "Sorry, sweetheart, but Nero has plans for this one."

Elias' head slumps as they drag him out of the room and snap the door shut.

"We have to do something," Sky says. "Please, we *have* to tell them."

"Sky, you heard Elias," I mutter. "You do that, and we all become expendable. Do you understand?"

Sky huffs, shaking his head in frustration. Lacy continues to pace. Occasionally she cusses under her breath.

A grueling twenty or so minutes go by, then the doors finally swing open. I jump to the bars as two new guards enter, dragging Elias by his wrists. He moans as the guards throw him back into his cell. There he lays, sprawled out on the floor as the door slams again.

I strain to see him, then I wish I hadn't and turn away. The sight of the cuts and bruises across his face and arms is burned into my brain.

Nero enters, glaring. "I should have known better than to try to break that one," he says. "EHC's have better breeding. But you three… you may be modified, but you're just a bunch of pathetic slags." He points at Sky and the guards fling open his cell.

"Stay back!" Sky shouts. "Don't touch me or I'll kill you!"

They grab him despite the threat, but he puts up a decent fight and grips the bars of his cell as they try to haul him out.

"Let go of him!" I bark, pressed up against the bars.

As soon as the words escape, one of the guards pistol whips me in the face. I fall back, the taste of copper filling my mouth. Though not as strong as Elias, Sky fights back with twice as much fury, but in a flash, the ops shock him into a lifeless lump. They drag him out the door.

Nero sneers. I spit in his direction, but it misses and the blood ends up on the floor. Nero scoffs and heads out the door, slamming it behind him.

Sky's muffled groans fade the further they take him from our holding facility. A sharp pain fills my chest and I slump to the ground, wiping my lips.

"Elias, are you all right?" I ask, not able to stop thinking about them taking Sky.

Slowly, Elias manages to pull himself into a seated position. He looks awful. Defeated. One angry cut sweeps across his right cheek, and the area surrounding both of his eyes is swollen and discolored.

"I'm okay," he says, breathless. "Sky... I know I don't know him that well... but I suspect they'll be able to break him if they do to him what they just did to me."

"All they have to do is show him his sister," I whisper, "and we're done."

CHAPTER 14

I have no idea how long Sky's been gone, but it has to have been twice as long as Elias.

"What did they do to you?" I ask Elias. Hopefully what he says isn't as bad as what my imagination is picturing.

"You don't want to know. It's better you don't." Elias takes a deep, raspy breath. "A lot of it was a blur. I blacked out."

Guilt racks me. "I'm so sorry, Elias. This is all our fault. We should have never let you get involved. Your uncle is gone, and now you're hurt, all because we brought you into this mess."

"I made a choice," he says, taking another breath. "All you did was push up our timelines. The EHC is to blame." He slowly pushes himself upright and grabs the bars of his cell, pulling himself to his feet. "I'll go out fighting if I have to."

Lacy scowls, continuing to pace back and forth. "I swear, if they hurt Drape—why haven't we heard anything about him yet? Do you really think they might have him in a med bay?"

"He's no use to them dead," Elias says.

Lacy's pacing speeds up and she's pumping her fists. She pivots and charges the iron bars at the front of her cell with a roar. She yanks and kicks at the bars until her hands go bloody.

"Lacy, that's enough!" I shout.

"This is all your fault, Fin!" She spins my way. "We wouldn't let you go it alone, and you knew it. Especially not Drape. He'd go to the ends of the Earth for you."

Anger burns in my middle at her words. How is this all *my* fault?

I push aside the feeling. This isn't my Lacy.

"You're remembering events incorrectly."

Her stare pierces through me. There's a storm brewing in her eyes. She huffs and returns to pacing. I slide back down to the floor. All I can focus on is Drape and Sky now.

The door to the holding chamber opens, and two operatives drag Sky in, sniffling and choking. Who's next? Me or Lacy?

Sky is tossed back into the cell beside me and his door is slammed shut. I don't bother to wait until the ops leave.

"Sky, are you all right?"

"No," he chokes out, forcing himself up into a seated position and glancing at the doorway Nero's entering through. Sky drags himself toward the door of his prison, gripping the steel bars.

"Please," he pleads with Nero. "Don't hurt her."

The door swings open again and a large, narrow capsule is carted in by two new ops. Almost like a large version of the mod kit, it's oval in shape and sleek lines run up and down its sides. There's a small window on the front. I gasp as Cia peers out of the glass. It must be protecting her from the radiation.

"Sky!" Her voice is muffled by the capsule's thick walls.

"No, *please*," Sky begs.

The ops direct the capsule into the empty cell to the right of Sky. He races to the bars splitting his cell and Cia's.

"*Please*," he says again.

"This is quite simple," Nero says, stopping at Cia's cell. "The mod kit, or the girl."

"Why are you doing this?" I ask. "We're just kids."

Nero turns to me and walks closer to my cell. "Stealing that tech and upgrading your genetics made you much more than a handful of slag kids. That stolen mod kit is worth more than your miserable lives. We do not take that sort of offense lightly, slag."

I have to keep him talking or something bad might happen. Time is all we have right now.

"You're going to punish *us* for *your* mistake? Maybe you need to look into your own people and find out how that kit was stolen in the first place."

He smirks and glances up at the ceiling, collecting himself before returning his attention to me. I can tell that one got to him.

"The EHC didn't spend decades perfecting our society just to have filthy dwellers freely mod themselves. There's an order to the world, and you stepped on it." Nero leans in, just out of my reach from inside the cell. "I have ambition. Goals. Once I clean up this mess, I will be done dealing with your pitiful sub-species."

"Just because you were born to the right family doesn't make you more human than us," I argue.

"Oh, that's where you're wrong, A298. Your freeloading ancestors stole enough from society to seal your fate. If you weren't capable of surviving pre-Flip, you weren't worthy to live on the surface. You're lucky robots are more resource intense than just churning out more miner babies or you wouldn't be worth the rations we send underground."

All I can do is shake my head in disgust. He's far less human than anyone down there. He has no soul.

A calm, content expression replaces the anger he'd shown just a moment ago. Nero struts into Cia's cell and presses his hand against a keypad on the doorway of the capsule. It lights up, and then the door opens. He grabs her neck and yanks her out onto the cell's floor.

Cia squeals in terror, shaking. "No! Don't! Put me back!"

It will only be a few minutes until she starts to experience the effects of the radiation.

"Put her back in the capsule!" Sky screams. "Please! Don't do this!"

The ops move to wheel the capsule from Cia's cell, and she races toward them. One of the soldiers shoves her, and she falls back in a heap. Cia pushes up, already scratching at her arms.

"You're sick!" Lacy screeches as Nero steps out of Cia's cell, closing the door behind him.

"No," Nero says, thrusting his thumb in Cia's direction. "But *she* is. It won't take long."

Confused, Cia rushes to the iron bars separating her from Sky, collapsing on her knees beside him. Sky reaches for her body and grasps her through the bars.

I glare at Nero. "You're just going to kill all of us if we give up that mod kit!" I shout, rising. "We're not stupid! There's no reason that little girl has to die! She's just a *child*!"

"You're right about one thing. There is absolutely no reason that girl has to die," Nero snarls. "But that is up to all of you. Go. Get. The. Mod. Kit."

With a wave of his hand, he commands his soldiers to follow him from the room. The door slams shut behind them.

"I don't feel right," Cia moans.

"I know. I know." Sky buries his face in her hair. "It'll be okay, Cia. I'm right here."

"My head hurts, Sky," she says, trembling. "I'm gonna throw up."

I bang on my cell door, the sound echoing. "Put an end to this, Nero! I know you're listening! This is *insane*!"

Suddenly, the doors of our cells, except for Cia's, swing open. Then a door on the far side of the room slides away, exposing us to the outside.

Sunlight pierces the chamber, and as if cued, Cia's screams pierce the air.

CHAPTER 15

Lacy practically jumps out of her cell like a wild animal set loose. "We can go!"

Cia whimpers and writhes as Sky squeezes her hands through the bars.

"Lacy, we can't abandon her," I say.

Lacy rounds my way and huffs. "Yeah, you're right, sorry."

"Help me up," Elias pleads softly to Lacy. Grabbing his forearm, she drags him to his feet.

I scurry out of my cell. Sky's on the ground, clinging to his sister.

"Sky…"

He releases Cia and races to the open door. Cia groans and stretches out her arms to him. He latches onto the bars of Cia's cell door and yanks with every ounce of strength he has. When it doesn't budge, he grunts in defeat and falls to his knees. Cia crawls over to the door and stretches her arm out between the bars to her brother.

Sky glances back at us. "Help me with the cell! If we work together, we can pull the—"

Elias reaches down, clasping Sky on his shoulder and shaking his head. "These are built to keep all classifications of citizens in. We won't be able to open it."

Cia abruptly yanks away from Sky. She falls on her hands and begins to cough and gag, eventually throwing up what little food was in her stomach, tears streaming down her cheek.

"I feel so sick."

"What can I do?" Sky pleads.

Ideas swirl in my brain. I analyze each option and project the outcome. Every single one of them is terrible and ends with one or more of us dead.

"We need to go get that mod kit for Nero," I say. "Come with us, Sky." If I can get him out of here, maybe it'll give us a chance. We can get the weapons and come back.

"You're out of your mind if you think I'll leave Cia here by herself like this," Sky snarls.

Cia reaches between the cell and touches his hands. "Just come back for me?"

I'm shocked by her bravery. Even she knows this situation is hopeless.

"I'm not leaving you!" he barks. Cia recoils, and Sky slumps with regret.

Pounding sounds from behind us, and I find Lacy attempting to break down the still-closed door leading deeper into the compound. When the pounding doesn't work, she starts swearing and yanking on the door handle.

"What are you doing?" Elias demands.

"We can't desert Drape." Lacy pounds her fist against the metal. "We don't know what they're doing to him."

They don't realize that if we waste our chance to get that bag, *none* of us are getting out of this alive.

"I'm staying here," Lacy says. "I'm sorry." Her eyes, filled with fright, focus on me. "I *am* sorry, Fin, but I'm not going with you."

"I can't leave Cia," Sky says to me. "I just can't do it."

"I know." I turn to Elias. "How much time do we... um, how much time does *she* have?"

He shakes his head. "I'm not sure, but based on how quickly she's deteriorating, not long. But you know as soon as we bring them the mod kit, we're done. It's a trap. They'll probably shoot us on our way back to the compound."

"Look at that girl, Elias, and then tell me what it is you want to do."

His attention darts in Cia's direction for a moment, then he looks down.

"Fine, stay here with Lacy and Sky," I say, frustrated. "I'll go get the mod kit. Maybe, just maybe, they won't kill me on my way back in, and, if we're lucky, he'll let Cia live. We'll worry about getting out of here later."

I make for the exit, but Elias grabs me by my arm. "I'm coming."

"You said yourself they'll most likely gun me down to get the mod kit," I argue.

"Well, then we'll just have to get gunned down together, won't we?" He lowers his voice. "Besides, if they do decide to ambush you, you'll need backup."

I take one last pleading look Lacy's way. *What if I can will her to come?*

She shakes her head. I know she's worried about Drape. So am I, but if she came with us, we might have a better chance of getting Drape out. But, just like I stood up for Lacy in the Oven, she stands up for him. Although she'd never admit it, she relies on him, too.

I whirl around and snatch Elias by the arm, pulling him through the released hatch of our prison. The heat bears down on my body. As soon as we step out, the hatch snaps shut. Good. At least Cia won't be exposed to as much direct radiation.

Elias and I hustle from the building. Soon enough, I spot the rock outcropping that we gathered at on the horizon, only a couple hundred yards away.

"Strange that Nero would just allow us go on by ourselves," Elias comments idly.

I gesture up. Two drones hover high above our heads, humming as their motors churn.

"Ah," he says. "Well, I guess we're not *entirely* alone then, are we?"

"No… Can the drones *hear*?"

Elias shrugs. "Speak lightly."

"I don't know about you," I whisper as we continue, "but I don't intend on dying today."

"Me either." Elias grimaces and stops walking for a second, gripping his side.

"You all right?"

"I'm fine… just give me a second." He takes several deep breaths.

"They knocked you around good, didn't they?"

"Yeah. Pretty sure I cracked a rib."

I offer for him to throw an arm over my shoulder and he accepts. "Lacy should have been the one to come with me. You and Sky are out of commission."

"I'm not out of commission." Elias starts walking again with my help. "But I don't need to overexert myself before we even get to the mod kit. Do you have a plan?"

"Well," I whisper, "the pistols are with the mod kit."

He smiles down at me. "That's what I was hoping you'd say." After a moment, he removes his arm from my shoulder, stretches, and then presses onward on his own. "So, you want to fight our way in. Am I right?"

"It's not like we have a choice. We go back with just the mod kit and we all become expendable. Cia dies anyway, and all of this was for nothing. If I could have gotten everyone to come, we would've had a better chance." The thought of Drape injured forms a knot in my throat. "But I don't know where Drape is."

"You two are close? You two and Lacy, right? But you haven't known Sky and his sister for too long?" Elias ventures.

"Very observant."

"So why are you risking your life for Sky's sister?"

"Isn't that what you did for us?"

Without a word, Elias raises an eyebrow and nods.

"This happened because she was trying to protect us. That's a brave kid who doesn't deserve to die."

"You know, I haven't been to this particular base, but the layout of this one seems almost the same as the others. If that's true, then the medical bay is just down the hall from the prison chambers. If we can fight our way through, we can save Drape."

It's a long shot, and unrealistic, but his words give me hope.

"Listen, Elias… your uncle… he wasn't in the cells—"

"I know. I don't know where he is. And if we go back, and we fight, we'll have to get out of there fast. There won't be any searching the whole base trying to find him."

Ahead is the rock formation. We pick up the pace. Cia doesn't have long.

"If there *is* a chance to go back for your uncle, know that you have friends who are willing to help," I say as we enter the space between the cluster of boulders.

"Thank you, Fin."

I peer through the cracks between the massive stones, eyeing the two drones following us. "How do we know they're not just going to fire down on us?"

"They won't," Elias assures me. "Not if we have the mod kit. It's too valuable. They won't risk destroying it."

We enter the opening to the outcropping and my eyes go straight to the spot the bag is hidden. A scurrying of footsteps just outside startles me.

Click.

I wheel toward the noise, my heart ready to explode in my chest. Half a dozen armed operatives race into the space. My instinct is to bolt, but there's nowhere to go. We're trapped.

They were tracking us the entire time. What all did they hear us say?

Several guards dart forward and grab Elias and me. My gut tells me not to resist. If we're dead, so are our friends. I tense as the group leader steps forward. He smiles, exposing a line of perfectly crooked teeth.

"Someone's been misbehaving," he scoffs.

I freeze. The op frowns and marches ahead, ending toe to toe with me. If not for my arms being restrained, I would try to punch that grin right off his mouth.

The man leans in, his stale breath overwhelming me. "Mod kit?"

I know there's no way out of this. Cia is dying, but something inside me is refusing to just give up. Standing my ground, I glare back at him. The leader cocks his head to the side and eyes the guard to his right, giving him a nod. The guard moves to Elias and delivers a powerful jab to his side.

Elias grunts and stumbles, but the two holding onto him won't let him down to his knees. The attacker lets out a laugh that sends a chill down my spine.

"Bet that rib's definitely cracked now," he taunts.

Yep, they heard everything we said.

"Is that all you got?" the leader questions, sounding disappointed.

"No sir." The goon delivers three more powerful punches to Elias' gut.

"Stop it!" I yell.

"Mod kit—now!" the leader barks in my face.

"It's over there!" I shout back at him, pointing to the loose rocks in the face of the stone foundation.

The leader motions to the man who punched Elias and gives him an acknowledgment. He rushes over, moves aside the rocks, uncovers the black bag, and carries it to his commander, who snatches the bag, opens it up, and shakes his head. He reaches into the bag, but instead of the mod kit, he pulls out a pistol and grips it by the barrel.

"Stupid traitors!" the leader growls, then smacks me across the cheek with the gun.

I scream, and if not for the two men restraining me I'm certain I would have gone down. Liquid drips down my face and splats to the ground, mixing into the reddish dirt.

"Just wait until we bring you to Nero," the leader says. "You're going to wish I'd shot you dead right here. Let's go!"

They start marching us back to the base. My cheekbone throbs. I'm confident my left eye is starting to swell, blood still dripping from my sliced skin. If I manage to get a hold of a gun, I will shoot all of his crooked teeth right out of his head.

Poor Elias wheezes, but I don't dare check on him. If we make it out of this, he'll have incredible damage to his chest and gut, and I have no idea how I can get him help.

At the outpost, the ops don't bother taking us in via the main entrance. They march us up to the hatch leading to the prison chamber. The door opens and the guards push us through, guns at our backs. Inside, another dozen operatives, including Nero, wait.

Lacy, Sky, and Cia rest with their backs against the door to Elias' cell. Cia's skin has a pale cast of green from nausea, and by the smell, she's definitely thrown up again. She rests on Sky's chest, her lids barely cracked. Elias and I have only been gone around thirty minutes, but she's certainly taken a turn for the worse.

Nero laughs as the ops who tracked us down close the hatch. "You're late!"

The man who pistol-whipped me steps around me, black bag in tow, and brings it to Nero. "Looks like they had other plans."

Nero rummages through the bag, grabbing the mod kit to examine it and ensure it hasn't been damaged. He handles a gun and inspects it before returning it to the bag, looking back at me. "And just what were you planning on doing with those?"

"Nothing, but I couldn't get the mod kit without getting them, too."

Nero shakes his head, still grasping the mod kit. "Right. You know, I was considering releasing you, sending you back to the hell hole where you came from, maybe even allowing that little punk to go home to Reso. But now? How can I do that when you think you can plot to shoot up my operative base and not face the consequences?"

None of us answer.

"Line them up! All of them! The girl, too!"

The guards swarm my friends.

"No!" Sky yells as he and Cia are yanked to their feet.

They drag the three of them toward us and force us all into a line. Sky carries Cia's nearly lifeless body. She's not even fully aware of what's happening. One of the ops draws his gun and aims it at us.

"Shoot the girl first," Nero says. "Put the poor slag out of her misery."

"No, please!" Sky pleads, wrapping himself around Cia, placing himself between the drawn gun and her, quite ready to take a bullet to the back on her behalf.

"You heartless leech!" Lacy shouts.

"Really?" Nero raises an eyebrow. "And here I thought I was merciful. What if we just wait until the radiation kills her?" He laughs. "Go on. Shoot the girl and her brother, then get rid of the rest."

I failed them.

Cia goes limp in her brother's arms. Teeth gritted, Sky thrusts an arm at the executioner. "She's only a chil—"

Bright light and thunder blow in the outer wall and I crumble into a heap. Chunks of cement fly in all directions. Dust blurs my vision. I fight to stay conscious as the world spins.

And then everything's gone. Everything.

CHAPTER 16

With a sharp inhale, my eyelids shoot open to a blurred world. I cough from the smoke and dust filling my lungs. Ringing pierces my ears as I place my hands on the debris coated floor, slowly pushing myself upward onto my knees.

Two versions of Nero lay flat on his back opposite of me, out cold. I blink several times and they merge into one. I study him. Like a good soldier, he's still gripping the mod kit.

Despite my vertigo, I jump up and snatch it, stashing the device in my pocket. Nero moans, and without a second thought, I deliver a kick to his head, ensuring he sleeps a bit longer.

"Jerk," I say, reveling in the minor victory when I hear a deep-throated groan behind me.

"Elias?"

His legs are buried, but it's no more than dust and minor rubble. "Fin?"

I race to him and wipe at the blood seeping from the side of his head, then dig around his legs to push back the heavy layer of dust and help him sit. Pain washes his face and he clutches his side.

"You alright?" I ask.

"No, but it doesn't matter." He scans the room. "Let's get out of here."

I pull him to his feet and spot one of our pistols, snatching it up. "Let's find the rest."

A moan sounds from the side, and I swing my attention to a soldier blown right into one of the cells. One of the mangled, busted bars pierces his chest. My stomach rolls over and I gag, turning away as fast as humanly possible. Across the way, Lacy and Sky have been thrown on top of one another during the blast. We stumble toward them, tripping on debris. I grab Lacy, waking her, and Elias does the same for Sky. As soon as Sky comes to, he jolts up.

"Cia!" he yells.

My heart leaps into my throat. "Be quiet!" I whisper. "These guards could wake up any moment."

"She's here," Lacy groans as she sits up and raises her hand to her head. Blood trickles from her eyebrow. The poor girl, coated in a layer of dust, lies just beyond Lacy, camouflaged in the rubble.

"Cia!" Sky yells, scrambling to her side, practically falling over as he trips through the rubble. "Cia, wake up. Cia?"

I lean away from Lacy and put my fingers to Cia's neck. "She's alive."

Tension falls from Sky's shoulders and he reaches under Cia's body, scooping her into his arms. Something shuffles behind us.

"Let's go," I say.

We rush toward the blown-out hatch.

"Stop, or you die!" Nero shouts, rubbing his head.

I turn to see five men plus Nero, their weapons drawn. The falling dust starts to clear. My mind reels. Escape or surrender?

I don't have a chance to do either as a blue arc shoots through the hole in the wall from outside, striking one of the waiting operatives.

I take my chance and bolt out the exit. Mason stands there, gripping a blaster. Behind him, a dozen fighters, all carrying weapons, head into the building.

"Come now," he says. 'We don't have much time."

"Uncle Mason!" Elias calls.

"Move!" Mason roars and rushes the group down a small slope toward a group of destroyed drones scattered about the outer yard.

"What's going on?" I yell as men in operative uniforms rush our way with blasters. More are armed with enormous weapons over their shoulders.

"They're with me." Mason stops, glancing back at the base, his expression frustrated. "Kid, what are you doing?"

I turn to see Sky on the floor, clutching Cia. "She's dead... I think she's dead."

We're all *dead if I don't do something.*

I snatch the mod kit out of my pocket and run back to them. I press it against Cia and set it off. Her entire body jolts, eyes shooting open. She gasps, but her head falls back as she passes out again. I have no clue if she's alive.

"Get up and go. Do you hear me?" I shout in Sky's face. "Don't get the rest of us killed."

He nods and lifts her up, rejoining our fleeing party.

Lacy trips and barely recovers. The blood on her head is still flowing. I grip one of her arms. Who knows how much she's lost.

"Elias, help me."

Elias does as I say and grabs Lacy's other arm. We lead her forward, after Mason. A loud alarm blares behind us as we dart to the far side of the base. Mason and his men herd us to a hanger, taking out the few men guarding the area.

"Establish a perimeter," Mason instructs his men. "I need a pilot on that craft getting it prepared for launch. Let's make sure we get our men before we go. Now move!"

Sky crumples to the ground, cradling his sister. Elias and I help Lacy sit and then I slump beside her.

Mason turns from his men to us. "Thank God," he says as he strides toward Elias, wrapping him in a tight embrace.

"Drape..." Lacy whispers, eyes pleading. "Fin, please, we can't abandon him."

"You know me. I'm not leaving Drape, I promise."

A tear drips down the side of her filthy face, leaving a trail in the dust on her cheek. "I know," she says. "But I can't walk anymore. The world is spinning."

I rise, looking at Mason. "My friend is still in there. I need to find him."

"There's no time!" Mason argues.

"You just ordered your men not to leave anyone!" I yell. "I feel the same way about my friend!"

Mason pinches the bridge of his nose. "Do you know his location?"

"Probably in the medical wing." Elias steps forward. "Not far from the prison chambers. Have your men cleared that area?"

"It's clear, but we haven't secured the whole base." Mason shakes his head. "You have twenty minutes. Twenty minutes, and this craft launches, do you hear me?"

"I'm going with her," Elias says.

Mason sighs and gestures to two of his men. "Jase, Todd, you're with them."

"Yes, sir!" the two men in operative uniforms shout.

Elias snags a blaster and I keep my pistol. After the day I've had with these leeches, I don't intend to shoot with a weapon meant to stun.

The four of us race up the hillside and into the now emptied prison chamber, our weapons drawn.

"Which way?" I ask as we pause near the door leading into the base.

"If it's anything like the other base I've been to, the medical bay is located just down this hall," Elias says.

"It's not," Jase interjects, looking forward. "This one is laid out differently than the ones I was stationed at. It's embedded into various rock formations. The medical bay is on the opposite end of the outpost."

"Well that's just great," I grumble under my breath. "We'll have to shoot our way in, won't we?"

"Looks that way," Todd says.

Elias defers to the taller, older man. "Let's do this. Jase, can you lead the way?"

"Yep," Jase says, and we move out into the first of many hallways. Jase assures us he knows exactly where the medical bay is. We enter down another dark hallway, the lights pulsating from the loud, screechy, emergency alarm system.

As of yet, we haven't run into any operatives. Hopefully they've already been taken out by the initial shootout while we were being rushed to the hanger. Unconscious bodies, hit by blasters, are strewn through the halls. I spot the lead operative, Mr. Crooked Teeth, lying in the hall. He obviously ran into the blast.

My trigger finger itches. My cheek throbs from where he hit me, and I have to admit, it's tempting. I know he's alive, hit by a non-lethal blaster.

It would be so easy.

I wave the thought away. We come to the back of the hall and Jase signals us to pause. He peers around the corner, then quickly backs up and shakes his head.

"How many?" Todd asks.

"Six—all locked and loaded," Jase whispers. "You three ready?"

"Yeah," Elias says.

"The medical bay is this way. If we can get past these six, your friend should be inside."

"Then what are we waiting for?" I ask.

"On my count."

My pistol is up. *We're coming for you, Drape.*

"Three… two… one—"

All four of us leap from our hiding place and fire. I'm a terrible shot, it turns out. I've only fired a blaster, and that was just once. I shoot off three rounds before I actually hit one of the operatives, but I do manage to take them out. Watching him fall is not as hard as I thought it would be. Today has dulled any empathy I had for the EHC.

Jase hits two guys, Elias one, and Todd takes out the last one. I'm thankful Mason sent more experienced shooters with us. I make a quick mental note that this is a skill I certainly intend to master.

"That shooting is bound to attract new operatives," Todd says, urging us onward. Jase leads the way to the end of the hall. Large metallic double doors stand between us and the medical bay. Using a keycard, Jase lets us in. It's a vast, long room with rows of beds on either side. Drape's lying with his eyes shut in one of the beds on the far side of the space. Hunched over him are three medical personnel, eyes wide as saucers. I hold up my gun.

"Run or you die," I hiss at them, pointing my weapon their way. They all dart out a back doorway in terror.

I race to Drape's bed and rip at the leather restraints tying him there. "Drape," I whisper, and his eyes open.

"Fin," he moans in pain.

"Easy. You're going to be all right. We're getting you out of here."

Jase and Todd get to work undoing the remaining straps. "You two," Jase calls to Elias and me, "guard the doors."

Elias hurries to the double doors we entered. I head to the doorway where the medical personnel bolted. It's here I spot a monitor along the wall, already logged in. I take a moment to snoop. A digital file labeled *EHC RESTRICTION PROTOCOLS* stands out to me. There's a holodrive sitting on the cramped desk by the monitor, so I snatch it up and raise it to the display. I glance out the door I'm supposed to be guarding, and since I don't perceive movement, I download some files. I press the button on the side of the device and holographic images appear above the drive as it downloads the files I select from the system. I'm not picky, downloading anything that causes me to raise an eyebrow.

"All right, kid. Can you get up?" Jase asks as he and Todd help Drape to his feet.

"Yes... I think I can walk. But I don't know if I'll be able to run," he says.

I smile. He's alive, that's what's important, and we have plenty of time to get back to Mason.

"Ops!" Elias warns, raising his blaster. "There's a whole slew of them coming down the hallway toward our location!"

"Go out the back way!" Jase bellows.

Elias and I flank Drape as we rush out the door I had been guarding. A single operative races at us from this direction, but Elias guns him down with the blaster.

A round of gunfire erupts from the double doors. "Todd!" Jase shouts.

Todd falls in a pool of his own blood just as Jase closes our exit and types in a code on the door to lock the oncoming operatives in the medical bay. Jase deflates as he glances down at his dead companion, but he doesn't waste time mourning now.

"Let's go," he says, stepping past us and avoiding the operative Elias knocked out. He leads us down a series of hallways and soon we're darting to the hanger. The craft is already started up, and most of Mason's men are rushing inside the open back hatch. Mason greets us just outside the craft.

"Todd?" Mason asks.

"He didn't make it," Jase says, his voice full of remorse.

Mason places a hand on the man's shoulder and tells him to get to the ship. He then gestures at us and guides us into the massive vessel. "Get inside. There's someone who wants to see you three."

Elias and I drag Drape into the hanger. The flying craft is close to ten times the size of the small hover car. I walk from Drape, who's leaning on Elias, and force myself up the ramp. Lacy, Sky, and Cia slouch in the row of seats lining one of the walls. They don't see me, but Cia is awake.

Finally.

Newly found energy rises in my body and I hurry to her, kneeling as I get there.

"Cia?"

She smiles at me. "Hi, Finley... I'm feeling a lot better now."

CHAPTER 17

I grip the side of the ship as it jolts a bit. The back hatch is still open. Armed fighters lean against the rear walls, ready to fire at anything that tries to stop us. One of Mason's men shoots down a few who made it within range. He leans his head to the side and speaks into the comm he has on his neck. "Give Mason the all clear!"

Almost immediately, the ship lifts from the ground, the back hatch closing. Lacy grabs me to keep herself from falling over, and while she's so near, I snatch her weapon. I don't really want her armed at the moment. Surprisingly, she doesn't even respond. It must be more important to keep holding onto me to stay upright.

"You good, Lacy?"

She smiles. "Are you kidding? We're all alive, you moron. Thanks mostly to you."

That's my old Lacy. Or a glimpse of what she used to be like before the mod. Like the girl who risked herself in the shipping area for Drape.

Elias stands across from us just as the ship jolts. Lacy grips me tighter and I snatch for a support beam on the interior of the ship.

"What's that?" I demand. "Are we taking fire?"

"Most likely it's my uncle's taking out all the ships in the hanger so they can't follow." Elias tips his head to Lacy. "You should get to the cargo hold to have her head checked. See if a medic can stitch up your cheek, too."

Not that he's in any better shape than either of us.

"You should, too," I say.

"I will. I need to talk to Mason first. Thank him for saving us and all." He smirks. "When you're done, meet me in the cockpit with that holodrive you snatched from the med bay."

"You saw that?"

"Yeah, and I'm sure my uncle would appreciate it."

I grin. "I'm sure he would. Meet you there in ten."

One of Mason's soldiers, dressed in an operative uniform, leads me to the cargo hold as I help Lacy limp beside me. Drape sits by Cia as a handful of men and one woman prick and prod at them to gauge their health. Sky waits nearby, a smile on his lips that's so full of love and adoration for his sister that it's infectious. My lips form into a grin. I can't believe we made it out.

"We have another patient for you," I announce, dropping Lacy off to sit by Drape. In a flash, I wrap my arms around his neck. "I was worried I might not see you again. How are you doing?"

"Better now." Drape grins and I snap back from him. He clears his throat. "They pulled the bullet from me, and they patched up my wound pretty well, so I suppose it could have been a lot worse for me." He looks over at Sky and sighs. "Let's face it, Fin, of anyone to have gotten shot, it's a good thing it had been me. If they'd drug me off and beat up on me like they did Elias and Sky... I'm not strong as them. I would have told them anything they wanted to know."

"You're stronger than you give yourself credit for," Lacy says.

"Did you just compliment me?" Drape asks. "You all right, Lacy?"

She ruffles his matted hair. "I'm just glad you're all right, Dope."

"I heard them talking. They were going to use me for experiments," Drape says. "They planned to see if they could reverse the effects of the mod kit. To un-modify me. I would have died from radiation."

"They're a long ways away from figuring that out," one of the doctors assures him.

Cia nudges Drape. "Be glad. Radiation poisoning wasn't fun." Her eyes sparkle as she looks at me. "Thank you."

"So the mod kit worked on you just in time then, huh?" I ask.

"It did," Sky replies for her. "Thank you, Fin. All of you. She's alive because of all of you."

As the medic inspects her head injury, Lacy stiffens in her seat. "Hey... what class of modification did you get, Cia?"

Cia tilts her head. "Class?"

"She just wants to know if you feel any different," Sky explains. "Are you stronger than you were? Smarter?"

Cia ponders for a moment. "No. I just feel like me... but my tummy hurts a little."

"Don't worry, sweetheart," one of the male medics says. "You're probably still experiencing the effects of the radiation poisoning. We'll get you back to yourself real soon."

The female medic eyes me and shakes her head. "You should be checked, too. I can stitch that up fairly quickly, if you'd like?" She points to my face and I instinctively reach up and touch my cheek. A small pool of blood forms in my palm. A part of me wishes I *had* shot that idiot who smacked me with our pistol.

"If you don't mind," I say.

She offers me topical numbing medicine, explaining it will require several minutes to kick in before she can start stitching me up.

"No, just go ahead and stitch me up. I'm in a hurry."

"Are you sure?" she asks, narrowing her gaze on me.

"Just work quickly, please."

She cleans and sanitizes my cheek, and then she works on the stitching. The sting of the needle makes me grit my teeth, but I've had my fair share of stitches. Mining will do that to you. No one down there ever offered me numbing medication though, so between that and my modification, suffering through these stitches is a breeze.

"There, only a few stitches," the medic says as she mists something on the wound. "This will keep it clean for now."

The unfamiliar kindness in her tone—or maybe it's just something about not having blood oozing out of an open wound—perks me up a bit.

"Thanks," I say, touching my fingertips to the wound. The mist has hardened slightly on my skin.

With a wave to my friends, I head to the cockpit. I enter the small, semi-circle of a room. There are three men and two women seated toward the front of the craft, working simultaneously on displays and controls. I assume one of them is the captain, but I'm not sure about the rest.

Mason stands with Elias and a group of three men. Mason's attention is entirely on his nephew, and he places a hand on his shoulder, giving Elias a smile.

A pang wells in my chest as I watch the two of them. Just like Sky and Cia, at least they know someone in their family. Before the last twenty-four hours, I'd rarely thought about where I came from. Who are my parents? Would they even know me if they saw me? What if I actually have brothers or sisters?

I wave off the questions. This was never something I had time to think about, so why should I start now? I have Lacy and Drape. They're my family.

"Fin?"

Elias snaps me from my thoughts.

"Looking good," Mason says to me with a wink. "I see they stitched you up nicely. How are your friends holding up?"

"Well," I say. "They're being taken care of, thanks to you, Mason."

"I'm glad we got there before anything worse happened." Mason nudges his nephew. "Elias here's trying to give me a heart attack, telling me what a close call you all had."

"Who are all these people?" I ask Mason while scanning the cabin. "An how did you break free and find us?"

He pauses, glancing at Elias. Elias nods at him and Mason turns his attention back to me. "I'm more than just a stubborn Noble class citizen looking out for defectors. I used to be an EHC operative. I've made many loyal friends on the inside. They helped me at that base."

I step back. "What? I mean, I figured you had connections, but I didn't think you were an *op*."

"I couldn't do it anymore. The people I hurt… the oppression… it was just too much." Mason's expression tenses a bit, as if he's reliving his past in his mind. "I made those connections when I was an operative. That network helped me start this resistance."

"How did you get away from being an EHC op?" I ask. "Getting out of that *club* can't be easy."

The tension in his face breaks at my stupid joke. "No, that '*club*' is normally a lifetime commitment. Elias' father was a personnel coordinator for the EHC. He helped me reassign my identity."

"Reassign your identity?" I echo.

"Every EHC citizen has a Society Placement Profile based on their lineage and class. Elias' father re-wrote mine. I was able to slip out of the system, eventually ending up at the Tenant class settlement. From there, I was able to build this resistance. It was tricky at times, but each of the former EHC personnel that fight with me were heavily vetted."

"So you have people embedded at the base they took you to?" I ask. "Is that how you broke free?"

Elias rests a hand on Mason's shoulder, answering for him. "Let's just say my uncle's personality and influence is contagious."

"Maybe so, but you kids put everything into motion." Mason grabs my wrist. "We weren't ready for this. Once I was taken, our allies had to leave their posts and gather at one of our safe locations. We're really scattered right now and need to regroup."

I nod and gently drag my hand away. He doesn't seem to notice my discomfort. I do trust him, but I have to consider my friends first. This rebellion is still new to me.

"Enough about me. Elias says you got information from the medical wing back at the compound?"

"Yes," I say, fumbling for the holodrive in my pocket. "I noticed they had restrictive files pulled up before the medical personnel panicked and took off."

"Well, let's have a look." Mason snags the device. "You never know. We didn't manage to infiltrate the medical wing, so you might have intel we don't have here."

He leads us to the right side of the small room and a large, half-circle desk. The equipment on this workstation far surpasses anything I've seen below ground. There are more displays and controls than I would know what to do with. He presses the holodrive into a slot and several images appear, floating above the desk.

"EHC Restriction Protocols?" Mason reaches out toward the holographic image again, selecting the file. The words *The Natural Modification Epidemic* followed by a tremendous amount of data appears.

"Natural Modification Epidemic?" I ask under my breath.

It's a lot of science mumbo-jumbo that, while I have been modified to a Noble, I'm still not familiar with. Mason runs his hands through his hair and pauses for a moment.

"If this is true, the dwellers are naturally adapting," he exclaims in awe.

"Is that possible?" Elias questions. "And modifying into what?"

"A resistant species. To resist the radiation and the new climate. They're doing naturally what people living on the surface use science to overcome." Mason's tone is practically giddy. "This is remarkable. Let's see…" He flips through additional information within the file, skimming faster than I can keep up with. "From what I'm seeing here, they believe in another generation or two the entire dweller population will be completely resistant. Unbelievable. Apparently all the tinkering they do in the Oven system to build better workers has hastened the process. Playing God by matching our genes for breeding has backfired."

"So… is it possible some of us already *are* genetically compatible?" I ask.

"According to this, yes. They're covering it up to maintain their workforce."

Mason flicks his wrist into the hologram to continue sorting through the file. A picture of the Oven—or one of the Ovens—pops up, and my stomach roils. I have to move back from the display. Before now, I didn't want to think about where I was born, it was too painful, but that pain has always festered in me, just out of sight. Knowing what I know now, I realize that that cruel system only taught me one thing: how to be a good slave to the EHC. It even bred me to be the "best" I can be.

My hatred for this system compels me to walk away, but the words *Preventative Methods* pulls me back in.

"What's that?" I ask.

Mason frowns. "They're trying to prevent the natural modification," he says, swiping at the documents. "Let me see here... just a sec..."

His lips silently echo his reading as he skims the data. A few minutes of silence are broken when he leans back from the holo-display.

"What is it?" Elias asks.

"They're testing fetuses at the orphanage system and destroying the ones that show evidence of these genetic markers."

"How are they even doing that?" I ask.

Mason leans in, reading. "Looks like they administer a specific medication under the guise of prenatal vitamins. It causes a miscarriage within a week."

Heat rises up the back of my neck. It makes sense. It's not like they're going to say, *Sorry, but your fetus is a threat, so it's got to go.*

Elias grabs at a paragraph in the holographic data field and it brightens. "What are 'inactive genetic markers'?"

"That would be fetuses that carry the genetic mutation to allow them to survive on the surface, but it's recessive. I imagine if you hit one of them with a mod kit..." Mason pauses and stares directly at me.

It clicks for me before he can piece together his meaning. "That's what happened to me," I say. "I carried the DNA to resist the radiation naturally, so shooting myself with the mod kit just amplified what I had. I was already resistant?"

"Recessively," Mason says. "You still would have fried up and withered like an un-watered shrub."

"Dwellers are on their way to becoming naturally equal with the EHC," I breathe, eyes wide.

"That's right," Mason agrees. "And the EHC leaders don't want anyone finding out." Mason detaches the holodrive and the holograms disappear. "Excellent work, soldier," he says to me.

"So what now?" I ask. "What's the point of having all the undercovers you had working at the operative base?" I jerk my thumb to one of the three men standing near us—the one wearing an operative uniform. The man smirks proudly.

"My uncle can't control where they get stationed, Fin," Elias says. "We're lucky a few were there."

"Like I said, we were months from making any sort of advance," Mason adds. "But you and your friends *modified* our plans." He smiles at his dumb joke.

"And what *was* the plan?" I ask.

"Basically, a governmental coup," Mason explains. "We have—or had, I mean—men and women embedded within the EHC networks on just about every base on the planet. There are hundreds of sympathizers—Century and Tenant class—all throughout the surface cities. We were waiting for the best possible assignments, the ones that gave us the greatest advantage. Now, we'll have to figure out what our next step will be."

I frown. "I'm sorry that we—"

"No apologies." He raises up the holodrive. "Besides, I believe I'm the one who owes *you* a thank you for this. This information could be the tipping point for the rebellion. It will force change." He moves his attention from me to the captain of the craft. "Take us to camp. We need to regroup and plan our next move."

Elias shoots me a reassuring smile. Everyone else seems very excited at the news, but I'm not so sure how I feel. I came to the surface to save a little girl, nothing more. Now it seems I've jump-started a revolution.

CHAPTER 18

From the cockpit, there's nearly a 360-degree view by way of the monitors and windows. We race through Reso, destined for Mason's hidden camp in the desert. I have no idea how fast we're flying, but it's definitely faster than the hovercar could go.

Reports have been flooding in via the monitors from resistance members within various settlements. Turns out the EHC didn't like our little display at the operative base. Big surprise. There have already been a number of sweeps in search of potential insurgents.

Shootings, arrests, and general lunacy have erupted thanks to the EHC's newfound paranoia. Pretty much every thirty seconds, soldiers enter the cockpit to give Mason a report on the events on the ground. I remain in the background, soaking it all in, dizzy with information. Lacy and Sky elbow their way in, both more alert than they were when we boarded.

"How are we going to fix this?" Lacy shouts, pulling everyone's attention in her direction. Her eyes have gone wild again, and whatever was driving her near madness has returned. I flash her the eye to shut up, but she's oblivious.

"Pardon?" Mason asks.

"From what I've been hearing since we left the base, the EHC has gone completely crazy," she says, fists clenched. "What do you think will happen to the *dwellers*?"

Mason frowns. "I'm not sure yet, Lacy."

"Well, how about I tell you?" she says. "Because if they're firing on their *own* citizens and making all these crazy arrests like your reports are saying, you best believe they'll rain hellfire down on our people."

Mason lowers his voice. "Lacy—"

"Don't *Lacy* me!" she hisses.

I grip her by the arm and she yanks away, bearing her teeth at me. She turns on Mason.

"Dwellers have been known to get shot or beaten just for *looking* at an op the wrong way. When word spreads to our home about what happened today, they'll turn those tunnels inside out. Dwellers can't protect themselves. We don't have guns. We're always the first to receive their wrath when things go wrong, and you know it!"

Mason sighs and locks eyes with her. "Lacy, I agree with what you're saying. The dwellers are in danger, but so is everyone else. *Including us*. It is

208

too dangerous to land this craft anywhere near your entry station. Our best bet is to regroup at our camp and move out from there. If we *can* help them, we *will*."

Lacy's nostrils flare and she inhales quick breaths. Her aggression seems to intensify with each passing moment she and Mason remain trapped in their stare down. At last, she exhales deeply.

"Fine," she relents and her eyes soften.

I inch to her and rest my hand on her shoulder. I don't dare speak.

"Um, sir?" One of the men manning the craft beckons to get our attention. "You should see this."

"Put it up on the display," Mason says.

A holographic image appears on the console. It's an underground entry station like the one we came from. There are mass numbers of EHC operatives gathering nearby, all heavily armed. If this is what it's like at a random entry station, I can only imagine how it is at the one *we* emerged from. Nero has probably sent twice as many men to our home as these dwellers'.

Lacy and I exchange glances. Her eyes are pleading, and I know that I can't stay quiet. There isn't time, not with the EHC jumping into action so quickly. It's true that I've never been particularly close with other dwellers apart from Lacy and Drape, but they are my people, and I have to have blood relatives down there—maybe even parents.

The EHC will be rounding people up like cattle sent to slaughter.

"You're a coward, Mason," I say, though I know it's far from true.

He turns to me, calm despite the insult. Elias, on the other hand, shoots me a look of shock.

"What?" Mason asks.

I shake my head. "I got that data for you from the medical wing. Surely by now they know what was downloaded. I'd bet my life that the ops will start rounding up dwellers with the inactive genetic markers. They'll kill them all just to keep people from… from having any *hope*. Now that this information is out, they'll massacre them."

"I know," Mason says. "But we can't—"

"No excuses!" I snap. "We have to act now, and you know it."

"Finley, I want to help the dwellers, believe me, but the ops are swarming the underground entry stations. If we go in now, we won't stand a chance taking them head-on like that."

Sky walks toward us from the doorway. He must have been outside. "What if there was another way in?"

"Another way in?" Mason echoes.

"Yeah," Sky says. "There's an alternate way in besides the station hub."

"Not possible."

"There's this underground habitat that people tried to build during the early days of the Flip, but it was abandoned at least forty years ago," Sky explains. "And it's no more than a few miles from the Slack's mining area."

"How in the world do you know about this place?" Elias asks.

"I used to go out scouting. My sister and I lived in the old subway tunnels. I'd go through old sewer and maintenance tunnels as far as I could, just trying to find somewhere to give my sister and myself a better life, when I came across the abandoned habitat. We came close to living there, but it was poorly protected from the radiation. I'm sure it's why it was abandoned. There were maps left in the habitat, and based on what I saw, I believe there are tunnels that lead to the surface."

"Or," Mason says, putting the information together, "tunnels that could lead us surface people down?"

"Exactly."

Mason brings his hand to his chin. "Everyone unnecessary for flight, please exit the cockpit. I need a minute."

On the way out, Elias grabs my elbow. "Why did you call him that?" he hisses in my ear.

"A coward?" I shrug.

"Yes, because my uncle is *not* a coward."

"I knew it would get his attention. Something needed to be done." Guilt for doing it gnaws at my stomach, but I felt like I had no choice.

Elias narrows his eyes at me and shakes his head. "I get that, but there are better ways."

Suddenly, the ship jerks and pulls to the right. We're changing course. The doors to the cockpit *whoosh* open and Mason stands in the entry.

"Get inside," he orders, rotating on his heels, not waiting for us. Lacy and Sky follow first, and Elias gestures for me to go ahead of him. Mason walks toward the craft's captain, and he looks our way. "Come here," he demands.

We listen. He means business.

Lacy smirks. "So what did you decide you're going to do?"

Elias throws her a death stare, so I punch her arm. I don't think Elias will let us verbally abuse his uncle anymore.

Mason ignores her and looks at Sky. "Can you lead us there?"

Sky nods. "Yes, sir."

∞

I gaze out the forward-facing windows as we approach what looks like an ugly crater in the distance.

"What the—" Mason says.

From the looks of the landscape, it had once been a city in the midst of the desert, like Reso. A handful of the surviving buildings near the edge of the crater appear as though they might pre-date the Flip. Tall, and with endless windows, the structures appear to be made mostly of cement. Everything now is made with metal or composites. These building wouldn't be habitable in the current climate, but the fact that they're upright is amazing. Tattered and crumbling, but upright. The variety in their designs is the complete opposite to the purely functional ones we saw in Reso. The once beautiful monuments are now a shrine to a past long gone.

We land alongside the massive crater and the men at the workstations pull up the 360-degree viewing screens. Something clearly happened here. A bomb, maybe? A small nuclear catastrophe? The way the windows are all blown out on the outer buildings and how the center of the city lacks any structures at all indicates an attack. Either way, the place is a ghost town, full of nothing but dust and crumbly concrete remains. The desert terrain ends abruptly once it reaches the crater, changing from yellowish sand to a hideous gray dust.

"Okay," Mason says as the ship powers down. "It's go time."

CHAPTER 19

We step through the back hatch into the wasteland of the once-substantial metropolis. Again, the heat hits my body and I'm reminded of how the surface differs from below ground in so many ways. We plant ourselves near the craft, gazing at the bombed-out city. It's quiet, but menacing in size. Even torn apart, I get a feel for how society prior to the Flip thrived.

A large container is carried down to the hover craft's entrance and Mason opens it up to reveal an assortment of weapons. He gives us all pistols to wear at our sides as well as blasters to carry. Knives are handed out, filling our belts to maximum capacity with weapons, flashlights, and gear. Mason helps himself to a few grenades, not offering us any. I glance at Lacy—probably a smart idea.

Lacy, Sky, Drape, and I are with Mason. We know the tunnels, so they'll need us. Elias also volunteered and insisted that he join us, despite

Mason's hesitation. A woman called Knuckles, who seems only a few years older than I am, is chosen to assist us. Apparently she's one of Mason's former undercover operatives. Then there's Jase, who's closer to Mason's age. Big and sullen, Jase makes me nervous. Since Todd was killed at the base he seems distracted—pacing, muttering to himself. But Mason knows him better than me, so I don't say anything. Mason chooses three more young fighters to accompany us: twins Oliver and Olivia, and a hulking man they all call Bricks. I can guess why they call him that, since he looks like a ton of them.

"Sky, you're leading point on this," Mason begins. "Can you locate the entrance into the tunnels?"

"That's the hope," Sky replies as he hooks his pistol into his belt. "I've done a lot of tracking living in the Slack. It's how we scavenged for supplies. From what I remember from the maps, we're searching for a marker called 'Hope's Gate'."

I gaze out over the demolished city. "Nothing here seems *hopeful* to me."

The whir of an activating blaster sounds from behind me, and I spin to find Cia gripping one like a miniature soldier.

Shouldn't she be on the ship?

"Cia, put that down!" Sky snaps, snatching the blaster from her.

"If I'm coming, then I want a weapon, too," Cia argues. Her feisty little attitude is evident, so she must be feeling much better.

"You're only going as far as the Slack, Cia, where I can hide you," Sky says. "Got it?"

Cia really should stay. Then again, it's not as if the hovercraft is well hidden. It would be just as dangerous to leave her. There are no guarantees either way, and I'm sure Sky doesn't want her out of his sight.

"What if we run into ops?" Cia asks.

"*Fine.*" Sky hands her a knife. "Keep it sheathed unless you need it."

She pouts, but grabs the knife and hooks it into her belt. "That's so dumb, Sky."

I snicker to myself. I like this kid. I glance at Lacy, who's admiring one of the pistols. "Blasters first, Lacy. Only use the pistol if you absolutely have to."

"I'll be careful, Fin," Lacy sighs.

"Are we ready?" Mason yells.

"Ready," Elias says on our behalf.

"You know it," Knuckles says as she finishes tying up her long braid. The hairstyle and her narrow face make her appear almost snake-like. I wonder how such a petite woman got a nickname like 'Knuckles'.

Entering the city is like walking into an alien world. Pathways line the buildings and smaller crafts dot everywhere we turn. The vehicles have wheels and don't appear to have the means to take flight. All the hovercrafts I've seen since surfacing have had similar looks to them, but each one of these is different from the last. Function trumps personality, I guess.

"There's no vegetation here," I comment.

"Don't be too surprised," Olivia says, gripping a handheld device in her hands. "The radiation here is off the charts. Like, this is *way more* than radiation from the Flip. This place was nuked."

"You'd think there wouldn't be any remains at all, then," I say.

Gray dust kicks into the air as we walk. Breathing it in makes my lungs feel heavy. Someone takes my elbow and I turn to find Drape, mouth open. I follow his free hand, pointing to a skeletal building. Poised in the doorway is what appears to be a statue of a man covered in black ash.

"What's that," I ask, trying to figure out what the big deal is, and the rest of our group glances in the direction Drape's finger is shakily pointing.

Bricks curses under his breath and steps toward it. "This has been waiting here for a hundred years," he says, reaching for it.

"Don't disturb the dead!" Oliver shouts.

Bricks' fingers make contact with the black figure, causing it to crumble away into dust.

The dead?

Bricks curses again and jumps back from the pile of black ash.

"What was that?" I ask warily, not really wanting to know the answer.

"A guy that got nuked a hundred years ago," Olivia says.

"Bricks, don't touch anything!" Mason orders. "You heard Olivia. The radiation here is high."

"It's off the charts," Olivia repeats. Her device produces a pinging sound. "Sir, we don't need to be here long. This stuff is dangerous... might even kill us."

Sky instinctually turns to Cia.

"I feel fine, Sky," she assures him. "I promise to tell you if I start to get sick."

"Keep it moving," Mason says, his blaster trained forward.

Sky nods and continues leading the way. Despite the damage, I can almost imagine what this place was like during the twenty-first century; full of people scurrying around doing whatever they did back then, oblivious to what was to come. They probably had no idea how good they had it before it was taken from them.

I glance at Drape as he shifts the blaster onto his uninjured shoulder, softly groaning. A knot forms in my gut and I touch his arm.

"You all right?" I ask.

"My shoulder still hurts," he admits. "I was... you know... shot this morning."

"I know. Drape, I'm so sorry. I shouldn't have—"

"It's not your fault," he assures me.

"But it is. I dragged you and Lacy into this. I made the call to run when they came in on us. It's entirely my fault."

"Well, then I forgive you, if you insist on blaming yourself," he says and winks at me. "Come on, Fin, do you really think I blame you? You're my best friend."

Warmth spreads across my chest and I chuckle. "Well, thank you. You and Lacy are my best friends, too."

"Guys!" Sky yells from the front of the line, pointing up at a tall structure.

"What is it?" Olivia asks.

"It's called a billboard," Mason says. "It was an advertising technique from pre-Flip."

The billboard stands ridiculously high, and half of it was blasted away by the explosions. There's an image of ancient luxury homes with the words:

The New Underground Safe-Haven: Hope's Ga

It cuts off, but based on what information Sky gave us, I'm certain the last bit of that was 'Hope's Gate'.

"Looks like we're getting close," Oliver says. "Which way?"

Sky goes still for a moment, considering our surroundings. "It should be just up ahead. Over that hill."

We continue down the cracked road until, as Sky predicted, we spot an enormous, rusted gate. Half of the gate is down, but the main entrance is upright. At the top of the entryway are the words *Hope's Gate*.

"Good job, Sky," Mason says, and with a kick, the twenty-foot-tall gate goes down shrieking, shattering in several pieces as it lands. Across the dusty yard beyond the gate is an enormous run-down building. Intricate and overly ornate, it was probably beautiful once.

"Looks like it used to be a resort," Bricks murmurs, then laughs. "Sure didn't survive the blast, though, now, did it?"

What's a resort?

The question doesn't matter, so I don't ask. Everything about this building looks dangerous. A part of me worries that as soon as we cross the threshold, the remaining walls will tumble down on us, kind of like the nuked person back there.

"Tread lightly," Mason warns as we enter.

Half of the ceiling is gone, allowing in rays of light that catch the dust floating in the air. The enormous lobby had once been well decorated with statues—no, not statues.

People.

My throat clenches. Some of them are huddled together in bunches. Others seem to have been frozen mid-run.

"Look at this one," Bricks says, pointing at a charcoal woman standing with her hands on her head.

"Bricks, I said no touching!" Mason shouts.

"I'm not!" he says, turning. The back of his blaster hits the woman and she falls apart. This time, though, instead of crumbling completely to dust, a few bones fall out and land at Bricks' feet. He shrieks and cusses again, his words echoing in the room.

"What did we say?" Jase snarls. "Quit goofing around!"

I move closer to Elias in the back, who's intently scanning every inch of the area. "Hey," I say softly. "What's the deal with Jase? He's not like the others. He's on edge. Is he always so serious?"

Elias lowers his weapon and looks at me. "He's been with Mason the longest. He was a lead operative before joining us years back, and he doesn't take honor lightly. Leaving his post was hard for him, even if it was the EHC, so he doesn't want everything he's left to be for nothing. Duty is all he knows."

I look ahead at Jase leaning in and grilling Bricks. He's a big guy—intimidating. The streaks of gray hair lining the sides of his head make him look older than he probably is.

"Check it out," Oliver says, interrupting the commotion.

There's a service tunnel bored into the exposed rock, spanning about fifteen feet high and across. We illuminate it with our flashlights. Maybe that leads down into the habitat Sky was talking about.

"Let's go," Mason says, taking the lead and leaving Sky to pull up the rear with me and Elias.

"I don't know if I gave you an honest thank you for all of this," Sky whispers.

I smile at him. "A thank you?"

He looks up ahead to his sister, skipping along like we're headed to a party. "For her," he says. "She means the world to me, Fin. If you hadn't decided to come, I would have gotten myself killed trying to save her. Then we'd both be gone."

"Of course. She saved us. It was only right."

I feel his hand stroke my arm. "I mean it, Finley. Thank you so much."

"Easy there, big guy," I say, playfully stretching my arm back. "Keep your head in the game."

I catch Elias looking at me. He must think we're so immature.

"I'm trying," Sky says, staring at me just a second too long.

Heat rises over my cheeks. *Is Sky* flirting *with me? Here?*

I start to say something, not sure what yet, and slam into Bricks. Yep. The man's nickname is appropriate.

"Watch yourself, kid," he says to me. I fumble out an apology, a little glad for the distraction.

"Why'd we stop?" I ask, peering around Bricks.

Ahead is an enormous crevice. I walk up and peer over the edge, and although I know it can't be, the abyss looks endless.

"How are we supposed to cross *that*?" Knuckles grouses. "This was a waste of time"

"Over there," Sky says, pointing a good ways down the lengthy, narrow stretch of the never-ending cavern. "A bridge with tracks. Like old subway train tracks, but way sketchier."

"No way," Knuckles whines. "There is no way I'm walking on that!"

Mason waves us toward the bridge. "Let's go check it out."

As we walk, my stomach rolls. In mind, I see nothing but crumbling tracks and our group falling to our deaths.

"The tracks were affected by nuclear blasts," Olivia reports as she checks her small device. "It could crumble."

"You're the blast expert," Mason says to her. "Can we walk on it or not?"

She taps the screen, studies whatever it says, and then walks to the bridge, bending down. "There's a lot of radiation in this cave, but the bridge seems sturdy. We got to go at it slow and easy."

Knuckles shakes her head. "That's nearly a quarter-kilometer long walk across an old, rickety bridge!"

I gaze down into the cavern again and listen. Soft *whooshing* sounds from the blackness. "There's water at the bottom of this. Rushing water." Now I'm picturing death by drowning. Nice.

"The pre-Flip refugees probably planned on using the river for power. It's likely there's a mill down here," Mason says. "Okay, cross or don't cross? Let's leave it to a vote."

I push away my negative thoughts. We've come this far, and I won't let the dwellers die. We *need* to warn them. "Cross."

"We should cross. You all know it's the right choice," Olivia says. Her brother and the rest agree.

"Form a line," Mason says, taking the lead.

I fall in behind him, the others at my back. The bridge and the tracks creak with each step. I wipe my filthy, sweaty hands on my pants.

"Slow and steady," Bricks reminds us, his voice shaking slightly.

"You scared of heights, Bricks?" Knuckles teases.

"Shut up," he snaps.

The bridge the tracks lay on is at least three or four shoulder lengths wide. It's not like we'll just fall over unless one of us gets ridiculously wobbly.

"Straight ahead, Bricks," I call back to him. "Don't look down or you'll make yourself dizzy."

Halfway across the bridge, a loud creaking followed by a *crash* and a splash echoes throughout the cave.

That doesn't sound good.

"Whoa, what was that?" Drape asks, his hands extended and knees bent.

The bridge starts to tremble. Our team freezes in place.

"Earthquake?" Jase suggests.

The rattle grows. We turn and realize what's happening.

"The bridge is collapsing!" Elias screams from the rear. "Run!"

The popping and cracking sends a jolt of panic up my spine. Bit by bit, pieces of the support beams start to tumble. Splinters in the cement below expand, forcing us into action. Mason nods.

"Run! Run!" Mason barks and bolts for safety. I'm right on his tail.

The bridge starts to sway. Mason's boots hit the earth and he swings back my way, extending his hand. I catch it and he yanks me forward, my feet hitting solid ground. I look back and realize we left everyone else in the dust. The bridge and all the people I care about is going down.

"Hurry!" I scream.

Faster than I've seen Drape run in his life, he pounds over the crumbling bridge. Face white with fear, he crosses to safety and collapses. Knuckles pushes in behind him, and right after her is Bricks and Jase. Sky yanks on Cia's arm, pulling her as they cross and tumble down beside us. The bridge jolts and Lacy, Elias, and the twins all lose their footing. One by one, they drop to their knees, fighting to regain their balance.

"Get up!" Mason and I scream in unison.

"Get up! Get up!" Cia echoes us, tears welling in her eyes.

My brain scrambles to work out a solution, but there isn't one. There's just no time. Setting foot on the unstable path could make the bridge disintegrate faster.

The four of them struggle to stay upright as the bridge continues to sway. Oliver and Olivia lean on one another, rising again. Elias is able to pull Lacy up and they all resume running. Mason and I wait near the edge, our hands outstretched. Bricks grabs me, anchoring me to prevent me from falling if I do manage to get a hold on one of the twins. Knuckles and Jase do the same for Mason.

Oliver extends his hand to mine and I stretch for it.

Snap.

The bridge jolts and the four of them drop. Like an avalanche of rock, the bridge crumbles piece by piece.

"Lacy!" I scream.

Elias slams right into Lacy, pushing her along the rock face. As if in slow motion, Oliver and Olivia jump. In my mind, I will them forward, but instead of their feet meeting the dirt, they plummet.

The bridge snaps free from the ledge. Olivia screams as she and her brother hang on to the broken, bent railing hanging below the side of the ledge. Elias has Lacy pinned against the rock face a few feet down, a hand on the fragmented track. Lacy screams as she scrambles for something to hold, but there's nothing there.

"Grab me!" Elias snaps.

Lacy wraps her arms around his waist to keep from sliding down the rocky wall.

"Get them up!" Mason roars, throwing himself to the edge, stretching for Elias.

"I can reach Oliver," Bricks says, pushing past me. Knuckles and Jase each hook onto Bricks' belt loop to keep him from tumbling over as he reaches down for Oliver. Below, the bridge collides with the water and interior of the cavern, the debris thundering as it hits.

"I'm slipping! I'm slipping!" Olivia cries out.

Oliver grapples for her. "Give me your hand!" he yells.

"I can't do it!" she cries and begins to slide. Olivia's fingers slip from those of her twin. Her screams echo as she falls out of sight.

Oliver's eyes go wide and he opens his mouth as if to scream, but there's only silence. A horrible *thud* sounds from below, and Olivia's terrified scream goes quiet.

"Grab him!" Jase roars at Bricks.

Oliver is frozen, but Bricks grips him and snaps him out of it. He's unwilling to move, but they drag him up.

"I can't get you!" Mason cries out to Elias. "Climb up higher!"

"I can't pull myself up," Elias calls back. Lacy sobs.

"Lose the girl!" Knuckles shouts down. "She's weighing you down!"

I reach out and seize Knuckles by her shirt collar. "Why don't we lose *you*!" I growl.

"Back off!" she warns.

"Don't drop me!" Lacy sobs.

"I won't drop you!" Elias shouts. "Climb up me!"

I stand over Mason and anchor him to keep him from slipping. Lacy slowly hauls herself up, using Elias' body to get leverage to reach for Mason. Mason stretches out to grab Lacy's arms and lifts her to safety. Without Lacy weighing him down, Elias pulls himself up to Mason and clutches his hand. Several of us help Mason hoist Elias up and over the edge, and he wraps his arms around his nephew, squeezing him.

Lacy's entire body is shaking. "You saved me. Thank you," she says, sounding more sincere than I've ever heard her be to anyone besides Drape and me in her life.

Mason steps back from Elias and swings his attention to Oliver, who's sitting on the ground, head hung. "Oliver... I'm so sorry."

Oliver wrings his hands together. "I couldn't grab her," he sobs.

Mason gives him a moment, but only a moment. "I need you to pull yourself together, Ollie. Can you continue?"

"Yes, sir," he says, but he doesn't move.

"Olivia was a good soldier," Mason adds gently.

Sky draws Cia in and leans slowly to look over the ledge. He squeezes his sister and walks to Oliver, offering his hand. It takes Oliver a few seconds to respond, but he eventually allows Sky to help him up.

"Let's just go," Oliver says.

And so we press on, led by Sky. His memory of when he scouted this area out is impressive. There are homes surrounding us, untouched for nearly forty years or so. There are trees lining the development. Confused, I walk up to one and touch its base, unsure how it could survive down here. I study it closer and notice it's made of synthetic material. Its natural appearance, with its abundant green decoration fluttering on its branches, is pretty, and something dwellers never see. It just reminds me of how little we really have working in the mines.

We continue walking through the habitat, passing unfinished buildings and pathways. Eventually, we get to a tunnel near the far side.

"I don't want to go in there," Cia says, clasping onto Sky's arm.

"It's ok," he insists. "It's just an old maintenance tunnel. If I remember correctly, we're getting close to the Slack. Just take my hand. I'll be right here."

She nods and he waves us forward. We enter the dark tunnel, sticking together. Our flashlights provide us some illumination, but the end is nowhere in sight.

It takes us about an hour to complete the tunnel, but the path opens onto an old, abandoned mining shaft. A busted, rusty gate conceals it. Sky throws it back and it whacks against the wall. The tunnel amplifies the sound, making me wince.

"This should lead us into the Slack," Sky says. He looks to his sister. "Once we get there, we'll find a safe place for you to stay, Cia."

Cia grunts, unsatisfied.

"Let's move," Mason instructs. "But be quiet. We're about to enter the home of the dwellers. There could be ops anywhere."

The shaft's air smells stale. There's no circulation here like there is in the newer mines. They fixed this problem several years ago after the EHC were losing too many of their workers to asphyxiation. We stick close together as we make our way down the narrow tunnel, taking several breaks to avoid getting lightheaded. This must've been a test shaft that didn't pay off. There are no signs of excavation beyond the one tunnel.

Soon, through the dim mining shaft, brighter lights flicker above us. Mason exits the shaft and the *click* of weapons fills the air.

"Freeze!" a voice calls out from the dark corner.

Bricks curses again. The man has quite a mouth on him.

"I know that voice," I mumble. "Yasay?"

The fat mining boss strolls toward us, about a dozen mining guards appearing to flank him. He chuckles when he sees us.

"Finley?" he questions. "Lacy... Drape..." He practically growls the names in our direction. "You three sure know how to cause a ruckus!"

CHAPTER 20

I lock on to Yasay. If looks could kill, I know he'd be dead. Too bad they can't.

"You three have really screwed things up, haven't you?" Yasay snarls at me. "Where have you moles been?"

"Listen, we can work this out," Mason tries to reason.

"Not talking to you, whoever you are," Yasay warns Mason, then directs a finger at me. His men shift with him, their guns directed at us, our blasters trained on them. "Finley A298—speak!"

Tension inside me twists uncomfortably. "Just Finley," I warn. The number system suddenly makes me want to vomit. Amazing what a little splash of perspective can do for a girl.

"You think you're a big shot now," Yasay muses. "Do you realize what you all have done?"

"No," I say evenly. "Why don't you tell us?"

"The EHC have tightened restrictions everywhere below ground. The ops have been crawling over the place the past few days. They executed one of my miners this morning—just a kid! Shot her in the head."

He says this with actual conviction. And here I thought Yasay had no soul. The ugly beast of a man shakes his head.

"And I know it has to do with you three!" He points a finger at me, then Lacy, and then Drape. "*You* stole *my* mod kit!"

I almost laugh, but I hold it in. "*Your* mod kit? Yasay, you and I both know you stole that mod kit. This is on *your* head, too."

He scowls. "They're not giving us any breathing room down here anymore. We were slaves, but at least we were oblivious to it. That kid they shot was twelve years old, and it was only because she looked like her!" He points in Cia's direction. "The ops are on edge, and that's putting us on edge, too."

"Yasay." I say his name with caution. We have a history. He's smacked Lacy around countless times, but we're still fellow dwellers. "I know you don't care for me, but I need you to listen to me. We uncovered something big. The dwellers are naturally mutating to resist the effects of the Flip, and the EHC are trying to cover it up. They have been for a while, but now they know the information has been leaked to a surface world resistance."

Yasay waves his hand Mason's way and laughs. "And is *this* the resistance, or whatever you call it?"

"A small part," Mason assures him.

"We're… mutating?" Yasay asks, as though the very idea, and me for believing in it, is insane.

"They've been destroying fetuses that show the genetic markers of a naturally enhanced dweller. Now that the information has been leaked, life will get a lot worse down here," I explain. "They'll start slaughtering people to make sure the enhanced genes don't spread."

Yasay's face goes slightly pale. The man has always been a slimy opportunist, but, as it turns out, he still has a speck of humanity. Or at least I hope he does.

He lowers his gun, motioning for his men to follow suit.

"Weapons down," Mason orders.

"Why are you here, so far from home, Yasay?" I ask as the tension lightens with the lowering of our weapons.

"We had to get out," he says. "The EHC has been pushing hard on all of us. I wasn't going to stick around for that crap. We've heard of shafts that lead out. Seems like you kids found it, too."

"Getting pushed around doesn't feel too good, does it?" Lacy mumbles.

"Don't get all sensitive A292. I had a business to manage. But now the EHC are hounding me, ordering me to double production." He gestures to one of his men. "Show them, Grant."

A man with a graying beard and soot covering his skin steps up and removes his glove, revealing two missing fingers. "They reviewed my yearly numbers yesterday," Grant says, staring at his hand. "It was a bit lower than they expected, so they decided to show what the proper response to not meeting their goals should be."

"That's how they want us running things now," Yasay says. "And I don't want any part of it."

"You beat people all the time for the simplest reasons!" I snarl. "Now you're just afraid for your own life. Don't give us that crap."

"I've had a change of heart," he says, forcing a sheepish grin.

"Whatever. It's simple; you need us, and we need you, Yasay," I say, not liking the taste it leaves on my tongue.

Lacy grabs me by the elbow. "Are you *crazy*?" she hisses.

I yank my arm away, maintaining eye contact with Yasay. "You know I'm right."

Yasay exhales deeply, then nods. "I know," he says, turning his attention to Mason. "Are you in charge of this pathetic, uh… '*group*'?"

"He's in charge of the entire rebellion," Elias snaps.

Yasay raises an eyebrow. "Nero Kyoto got here several hours ago. The man's out of his mind.

235

Furious. Apparently there was an attack on an operative base—" Yasay pauses, seemingly judging our reactions. "Did *you* attack an operative base?"

"What can you tell us?" Mason asks, drawing him back in.

"There has to be at least thirty or more ops around the mining operations, the Oven, and the living sector."

"Then that's what we should take care of first."

"Is there a way we can sneak up on them?" Elias asks.

"Most of them are gathered in the main cavern, outside the operations center right now," Yasay explains.

"Then we can use the mine tunnels and the Slack to our advantage," I say. "Go in from different angles. Swoop in from the tunnels."

"We must attack at the same time," Mason adds. "We need a way to radio in to one another when we're all in position."

"I brought a radio," Yasay offers as one of his men hands over a set of two-way radios. "These will do. We can divide into two groups and charge in."

"We have to go in hard and quick," Mason instructs. "And avoid hitting dwellers. No civilian casualties. These people have suffered enough. My men must use blasters."

"Yes, sir," Elias says.

Mason points at Yasay, who hands Mason a radio. "You and Fin lead up one troop. I'll lead the other."

"I'm going with Fi—" Sky starts.

"No," I interrupt. "You, Drape, and Cia stay here, where it's safe. There are too many operatives to hide her in the Slack now. Cia is too young to get involved in this, and Drape is hurt."

"I'm fine!" Drape insists.

"No, you're not," I shoot back. "You three need to stay here. If things go south, find another way and get back to the hovercraft—alert the rest."

Drape starts to argue again, but Sky holds up his hand.

"Okay. Drape and I can handle it back here," Sky says, then eyes his sister. "Take care of Cia."

The little girl huffs. "I'm not a baby," she mutters.

Half of Yasay's men go with Mason, Elias, and Lacy. Jase, Oliver, Knuckles, and Bricks, along with the second half of Yasay's dirty dozen, go with Yasay and me. I signal to Sky, Drape, and Cia before Elias and I lead our group down our mining tunnel. Drape is still sulking.

It doesn't take us long to reach our destination just inside one of the mining tunnels with a view out into the very center of the cavern. The entrance to the Oven waits on one end. A group of frightened dwellers are lined up against the face of the building. Men shout something about testing.

My stomach roils as I realize the EHC are prepared to execute anyone who tests positive for the genetic markers, and the dwellers in line outside the Oven probably have no idea what's happening.

On the opposite side of the massive opening waits the wide tunnel leading into the living space.

"Why are you doing this? Please, don't shoot me!" a man's voice sobs.

In one corner, a huddle of miners are being held up at gunpoint. One man sits on the ground, his ear bloodied, several operatives looming above him.

Anger burns in my chest. The ops have always abused their power over us, but this is an entirely new monster.

"Radio Mason," I say to Yasay.

"Mason," Yasay says. "We're in position."

The two-way beeps softly. "Get ready to run on my count," Mason's voice whispers through the speaker.

On Mason's count, Yasay and his men suddenly push in front of me.

"Watch it, buddy," I mumble.

In a flash, they toss several small metal objects down into the crowded opening. Loud, unsettling explosions detonate ahead of the Oven. I cover my head, my body riddled with fear, and glance back up.

Yasay meets my eyes as the tunnel fills with dust from the explosions. The Dwellers are gone.

He just killed all those innocents along with the ops. I can barely breathe.

"What are you *doing*?" I growl.

He bares his teeth at me in a sort of twisted smile. There's no time to try to reason with Yasay's lack of morals. I raise my weapon, wanting to point it at him, but instead I ready myself to advance.

CHAPTER 21

Smoke is thick in the air as shots skim past us and rip into the cavern's surface.

"Return fire!" Mason's voice echoes from the radio as his team fires back from their tunnel.

I shouldn't have split up from Lacy and Elias. All we've done is divide our team. What if we hit our friends in the crossfire? My enhanced intelligence is not helping me with battle strategies whatsoever. I should've gone with my gut.

"Push them back!" I order my team, and Yasay nods in agreement.

We manage to cut off the surviving operatives from escaping by way of the tunnel networks and instead back them toward the exterior of the Oven. Surviving Dwellers race our way and we make room for them to pass, but no op dares make such a risky move.

"Keep moving in on them!" Mason shouts as his team emerges from their tunnel, working operatives back and away from the escape tunnels.

Our company tucks into several rock formations and behind mining equipment for cover. The ops, on the other hand, are exposed. They frantically search for cover and fire aimlessly back at us. They have no choice but to stand outside the Oven and try to fight their way out. Several ops fall back behind narrow stalagmites in front of the complex. The structure is built into the rock wall, so there's no back exit.

Gunfire *cracks* from the right and left. I check the juice on my blaster, finding it's almost dead. I know I'll eventually have to use more deadly force. I make my way to a large boulder and glance up. Lacy is about fifty yards from me. She's safe, and fighting like a natural soldier, although her aim is about as great as mine. When this is done, we have work to do.

Both teams, mine and Mason's, continue firing on the Oven. By some miracle, we're able to keep the EHCs pinned down. To attempt to win themselves a little ground, the EHC operatives start firing flash rounds. The bursts of light blind us for a few seconds and throw us off our momentum. Yasay makes a motion, darting in my direction as two of his guys provide cover fire. He slides behind my boulder, nearly ramming into me.

"Who knew you'd make such a good soldier, girly," he growls.

"Who knew an old bag like you'd have any moves left," I snarl back, glancing past the boulder and firing aimlessly into the smoke.

The radio at Yasay's side crackles and Mason's voice comes through. "They might be using the cover smoke to retreat—don't allow it!"

Yasay grips the radio. "I want my guys to charge the place on my go!"

"Whoa, bad idea!" I snap.

Yasay doesn't have the chance to argue with me since Mason's angry shouting reverberates through the two-way.

"Ignore that order! I repeat, *ignore* that order!"

Yasay grips the radio. "These aren't your men, Mason! On my go, boys!"

"Yasay, don't do this," I plead.

He slams the radio down beside me and waves to his men. They charge as the dust and smoke start to clear. They reach the operatives before they have a chance to fire on them, but what Yasay doesn't realize is that most of them are Century class leeches. They're stronger and better trained. Going hand to hand doesn't work in fighting modified soldiers.

This will be a bloodbath.

"Forward!" I command to the remaining members of my team.

From the opposite side, Mason calls out the same order to his group. It's all or nothing now.

Just as I get to the outer structure where the bulk of the fighting is taking place, Nero Kyoto emerges from within the Oven, a scowl on his face. My heart jumps into my throat and he whips out a small knife with a shiny, charcoal-colored blade.

Two of Yasay's men go after him, and in one swift motion, Nero slices each of their throats, letting them fall. He hardly took a breath to accomplish the gruesome task. My brief encounter with him in the subway tunnel didn't prepare me for this. I had no idea what we were dealing with as far as Nero's physical abilities were concerned. He's clearly been trained by the best.

Lacy falls in beside me. "Nero," she seethes. She rushes ahead of me, her pistol now drawn after tossing her blaster aside, firing frantic shots toward him.

Nero takes three swift steps back, avoiding her shots. He moves for the gun at his side, but Lacy is on him too quickly. She slams into him, pistol in hand. His own weapon is knocked from his hand and slides across the rocky earth, but he restrains her to keep her from firing on him. In one quick motion, Nero pulls a swift wrestling move on Lacy. He lifts her up above his head and tosses her against a massive stone like a rag doll. I glance back for a brief second to see that Mason, Elias, and the others are busy with their own problems.

It's just me.

Nero sees me and leaps up onto a huge stone. I slide to a stop, but it's too late. He throws himself off the boulder, over Lacy, and right into me. His heavy body slams into mine like a wrecking ball, throwing us to the ground. Pain races up my back.

"This is your fault, you know?" he taunts as he grabs my wrists. I flail, trying to free myself, but it's useless. "Lots of people will die because of *your* stupidity. You couldn't just fall into line like everyone else, could you?"

He raises the blood-coated knife. I grit my teeth in expectation of what's to come, but something slams into us, pushing me down. Nero flies back and I watch him and Lacy tumble down the slight slope at the base of the Oven's exterior structure. I scramble to my feet and see Nero upright and delivering a swift kick to Lacy's side. He glares up at me, gasping for breath. In his hand, he still grips his bloody blade. I snap my attention to a very still Lacy and the blood seeping into the front of her shirt.

"Lacy!" I scream. Without hesitation, I charge Nero. My fists fly into his nose, and despite my smaller frame, Nero retreats slightly.

"Where did a useless dweller learn to fight?" he snarls, wiping the blood from his nose. He swings his blade at me and I lock onto his wrist and spin on my heel. I twist his elbow and, with the knife in his hand, pierce him in his gut. He releases his knife, so I take the opportunity to push it in further.

He falls to his knees in front of me as I twist the blade and then release it, leaving it protruding from his stomach. There's more shock than anything in that gaze of his.

"I am not a dweller anymore."

He falls, writhing in pain as the critical gash bleeds out. There's a part of me that wants to finish him off.

I rush to Lacy, scooping her limp body into my arms, cradling her close.

"Lacy," I sob. "You can't die."

Someone touches my shoulder and I flinch. Turning, I find Mason standing beside me, concern filling his face. On his tail, Elias rushes in our direction.

"Is she alright?" Elias asks, voice laced with panic.

Holding Lacy, I glance back and see that Mason's men have at last gained control. They charge in and pin down op after op. Part of the EHC refuse to surrender. Jase has no remorse as he shoots one in the head and moves on to the next. They're either killing or restraining the last of the operatives now.

Turning back to Nero, my mouth drops. He's not breathing—he's lost too much blood. I killed him. taking a life is hard no matter who it is, but he can no longer hurt us Dwellers anymore.

It's over, we've won, but now all my attention is focused on my closest friend. I touch Lacy's neck, searching for a pulse. My own heart leaps when I find one. It's weak, but there.

"She needs medical attention right now!" I yell.

Yasay clears his throat from behind us. He and his men have guns pointed at us—all of us. There are only eight of us, but nine of them who survived.

"What is this?" I hear Knuckles sneer.

"Yeah, put those weapons away!" Jase shouts.

Yasay laughs. "Thank you, Mason, for helping us solve our EHC problem. Now I'm going to need A298 to hand over that mod kit she stole."

I carefully lay Lacy's head down and rise, staring Yasay down. "Lacy needs a doctor,"

"Now," he snarls.

"No," I say.

He points his pistol my way. "I won't ask again," he warns.

"Shoot me, and you'll never find it."

"You don't have it on you, then?"

"No."

"And I'm guessing you're just too noble to give up its location?"

I cross my arms and scowl. He shakes his head, and, not missing a beat, fires his gun.

"No!" Elias screams.

I round and watch Mason tumble over, having taken a direct shot to the skull. Elias' uncle is dead before he even hits the ground. My jaw drops, and I quiver in shock.

"You bastard!" Elias snarls. He charges Yasay. Before he can reach the coward, one of Yasay's goons shoots one of our blasters, knocking Elias back. He falls down rolling and moaning.

"Don't!" I hiss when the man raises the blaster again.

"The mod kit," Yasay says to me, shifting his gun to Knuckles. The woman stiffens. "Or I shoot her. I wouldn't hesitate, A298. There are plenty of your little rebel friends I can start picking off if you do."

"Okay." I raise my hands in the air a little. "There's no need to kill anyone else."

"That-a-girl," he says.

The earth quakes a bit, and he points his gun at me as though he thinks I'm responsible.

I raise my hands higher. "That's not me."

A hoard of people charge into the cavern from the three exit tunnels. Two familiar faces lead the groups from each tunnel: Drape and Sky. There must be close to fifty or more men and women swarming the area from all directions, most armed with mining equipment while others are sporting stolen guns.

"Put your weapons down!" Sky's voice echoes in the cavernous opening. "Right now, or you're done! Put your guns on the ground!"

With no alternate way out, Yasay and his fighters surrender. Just as Yasay lowers his pistol and places it down, Elias rises. He lunges at Yasay, throwing a powerful punch into the man's jaw. Yasay spins and crumbles, knocked out completely. Elias pounces on his lifeless body like a wild animal, ready to rip him to shreds.

"Elias, that's enough," Bricks growls. He and Jase yank Elias off the unconscious Yasay. "We're not the EHC. He will pay for what he did, just not like this."

Once back on his feet, Elias yanks from their hold and runs to Mason's side, sobbing hoarsely over his uncle. Clutching Mason's shirt, Elias lifts him until their foreheads meet. He wraps Mason's limp frame in his arms. My heart aches for him as I turn and hurry back to Lacy. Drape's not far behind.

"Medic!" I call out to the crowd.

Two men hurry to us. Lacy quietly moans as Drape and I cradle her. The men kneel around us, and one tears the bottom half of Lacy's shirt open to gain access to the wound.

"She'll be fine if we hurry," one of them says. He looks to Drape and the other man. "Help me carry her into the Oven to the medical wing."

The three of them lift her and rush her inside. Lacy's blood stains my hands. I wipe it onto my pant legs as I rise from my knees. I want to follow her in, but we're not done here. Sky approaches me, putting his hand on my shoulder.

"Couldn't just sit still, could you?" I ask.

"No," he says. "We rallied as many people from the Slack as we could. It didn't take much to get them moving. I just told them what the EHC's plan was for the dwellers."

The sheer number of people who came gives me hope, until I see Elias; alone, hugging himself as Jase and Bricks gently lift Mason.

"I need to talk with him," I say to Sky.

"Yeah. I better keep an eye on Cia, anyway."

I walk to Elias' side. He doesn't notice, so I touch his arm. Muscles tenses under my fingers. Elias drops his hands to his sides and hangs his head, tears staining his cheek. I search for the right words, but none measure up. I hug him, and instead of tugging away like I expect, he melts into me.

"I'm sorry," I whisper.

He squeezes me, releasing the emotion of the moment, then pulls back. When he does, sweet Cia rushes over and wraps her arms around Elias' waist. He manages to crack a shaky smile down at her, despite his teary eyes.

I go toward one of the outer tunnels with a rocky ledge overlooking the cavern. I climb up, and Sky follows me. We reach the peak several yards up, and people look up and stare in our direction. Sky stands just to the left of me.

"What are you planning to do?" he asks.

"Speak."

I reach into my pocket and produce the mod kit. Despite what I told Yasay, I've had it on me the entire time. It's too valuable to risk hiding it down here. I raise it up high above my head.

"We are naturally adapting to go back up top!" I shout, and the crowd grows silent. "And the EHC doesn't like it. We are becoming stronger, resistant, and it terrifies them. It threatens their way of life."

I scan the people in the crowd. I don't know if I know any of them, but in the end, this *is* my family.

I lower the hand holding the mod kit. I know it might not be safe, but at this point we're all going to die if we do nothing. "Well, you know what? Too bad. Because their way of life isn't working for me—for *us*—anymore. I say that it's time we speed up the process."

After a slight pause, the crowd erupts into a cheer. My body tingles with energy; the energy of hope. I look to Sky and his lips form a wide grin. I gesture for the crowd to quiet down.

"Come forward, and to anyone willing to join the fight, I'll modify you today so you can go up top and free us all!"

A handful step back, fearful. I understand that, but the overwhelming majority charge to the base of the ledge. Shouts echo from the crowd.

"I want to fight!"

"Modify me!"

"I'll go!"

Sky puts his hand on my shoulder and gives me a nod of approval. I look to the tunnel that leads to the caverns, our way out to the surface.

"It's time!" I yell to the crowd, raising the mod kit high above my head for all to see. "It's time we bring the fight to them!"

The End of Book One

∞

Exclusive Updates on Book 2 as well as free content: Be the first to find out when book two of the Manipulated series will release. In addition, get free content, giveaway opportunities, and other exclusive bonuses by joining my VIP List on Harper's web site.

www.harpernorth.com

Thank you for reading Modified, book one of the Manipulated series. If you enjoyed reading this book, please remember to leave a review on Amazon. Positive reviews are the best way to thank an author for writing a book you loved. When a book has a lot of reviews, Amazon will show that book to more potential readers. The review does not have to be long—one or two sentences are just fine! I read all my reviews and appreciate each one of them!

www.harpernorth.com

Acknowledgements:
Special thanks to Torment Publishing! Without you this book would not have happened. I love you guys.
Thanks to all the early beta readers and the support of my fans.
Thanks to all my family for the support!

Credits:
Chase Night - Editor
Jack Llartin - Editor
David R. Bernstein - Publishing & Marketing Support
Jenetta Penner - Publishing & Marketing Support

Made in the USA
San Bernardino, CA
10 December 2017